The intruder fumbled at the door lock, and Becky slipped out of bed and lit a lamp. Grasping the pistol tightly, she moved into shadows before the door opened. In the dim light, she recognized Oliver Stover. He peered into the cabin, his eyes flaming when he saw her pressed against the wall.

Reaching for her, he said, "Now we can continue what your big brother interrupted a few months ago."

"Stay away," Becky warned as she lifted the pistol, but Oliver laughed derisively. Becky tried to break his grasp on her arm, and screamed when the gun discharged right beside her head.

More Meadowsong Romances for your reading pleasure:

BY Irene B. Brand:

The Touchstone
Freedom's Call

FREEDOM'S CALL

IRENE B. BRAND

Power Books

Fleming H. Revell
Old Tappan, New Jersey

Scripture quotations are from the King James Version of the Bible.

Library of Congress Cataloging-in-Publication Data

Brand, Irene B.
    Freedom's call / Irene B. Brand.
        p.   cm.
    ISBN 0-8007-5346-1
    I. Title.
    PS3552.R2917F74   1990
    813'.54—dc20   89-70075
                                                              CIP

Copyright © 1990 by Irene B. Brand
Published by the Fleming H. Revell Company
Old Tappan, New Jersey 07675
Printed in the United States of America

TO
The Dady clan

"Eastward, I go only by force,
but westward I go free."

HENRY DAVID THOREAU

FREEDOM'S CALL

1

With three melodious blasts of the *Allegheny's* whistle, Matt Miller announced the packet boat's arrival at Gallipolis, Ohio. Becky Nelson stood beside her brother in the pilothouse and stared intently at the city square surrounded on three sides by brick structures. Her hands pushed nervously at the long, blond hair falling around her shoulders, and she squeezed Fluff so tightly that the Maltese dog yelped his displeasure.

"Sorry, Fluff," Becky murmured, and seeking to shield her body behind Matt, she peered around him to see if she could spot Oliver Stover in the crowd gathering on the brick wharf. She darted a quick look at Matt and realized that he hadn't forgotten about the Stover episode either, for although his hands steered the boat expertly against the wharf and reached upward for another pull on the whistle, he said quickly, "I don't think you should be up here in plain sight, Becky. Go below."

Resenting Matt's domination, Becky still obeyed him without question. Slipping down the ladder, she entered the galley to find Aunt Lizzie taking a pan of corn bread from the oven. Scrawny, wiry, and wrinkled Lizzie Brannan, once their neighbor in Pittsburgh, had served the last five years as the *Allegheny*'s cook. During that time she'd doubled as Becky's confidant, giving her a break from the all-male atmosphere of the boat.

"Why are you wearing a bonnet?" Becky asked her friend as she accepted a chunk of hot buttered corn bread. Setting Fluff in his box behind the stove, Becky blew on bits of the bread and dropped them beside the dog.

"I'm fixin' to go uptown as soon as this boat is unloaded. Supper's ready for the men. You know I've got a cousin in this town, and I'm going to spend the night with her."

"I wish we hadn't stopped here, Aunt Lizzie."

"Why in tarnation not? We always do." Then seeing the worried expression on Becky's face, Lizzie said understandingly, "You mean because of that fracas with Oliver Stover, last trip?"

Becky nodded. "The Stovers are such influential people in this area. I'm afraid they'll try to get even with Matt."

"Oh, they ain't so influential as you might think. Most folks in this area ain't forgot that Oliver's old grandpappy stood with the British in the Revolutionary War—hand in glove with that Hair-Buyer Hamilton who incited the Indians in the Northwest Territory."

"But that was such a long time ago. Oliver won't be blamed for what his ancestors did."

"Well, I hear tell the Stovers are still ready to do the British a good turn when they can. So I wouldn't worry about what Matt did to him. That young smart aleck Oliver is always getting into some kind of trouble."

"Yes, but he was furious when Matt knocked him in the river and left him adrift down below the Scioto River. And I don't blame him. The man only tried to talk to me. I avoided him, but you know Matt."

Lizzie laughed as she picked up a little satchel. "Yeah, I know Matt. After he started this packet-boat business, five years ago, in eighteen thirty-nine, to get you away from the men at Pittsburgh, he ain't about to let some scalawag like Oliver Stover get familiar with you."

"But I can't understand it. Why does he treat me like that? I'm twenty years old—most girls are married by this time. Do you know why Matt won't let me keep company with a boy?"

Lizzie's faded brown eyes failed to meet Becky's gaze. "Yes, I know, child, or at least I *think* I do, but I ain't going to tell you. Just be thankful that Matt looks out after you. Many a young woman has fallen into hard times when she didn't have anybody to protect her. Matt Miller is pig-headed, but he loves you in his own peculiar way."

Matt, her only relative, had become Becky's guardian when their mother died several years ago. Fifteen years her senior, short, stocky, swarthy Matt favored his German ancestors. After the death of Matt's father, his mother had married a Norwegian sailor, who soon deserted her, leaving Becky as the only reminder of a short, stormy marriage. Of course, Becky couldn't remember her father, but she'd inherited the blue eyes, fair hair and skin, and the lithe form of her Scandinavian forebears.

"I'm getting tired of being treated like a child, Aunt Lizzie, and one of these days I'm going to break away from Matt. You just wait and see."

"Yeah, you've told me that before." She patted Becky on the cheek. "Be careful tonight, child. I'll be back early in the morning."

Fluff's startled yelp brought Becky awake in a hurry, and she sat up in bed, still groggy with sleep. Darkness surrounded her. Listening intently, she heard stealthy footsteps outside the door.

A quiet call filtered through the panel. "Becky?"

Was that Oliver Stover? Becky hadn't heard his voice often enough to recognize it. She reached for the loaded pistol Matt insisted that she keep by her bed, and knocked on the paneling between her cabin and Matt's.

The intruder fumbled at the door lock, and Becky slipped out of bed and lit a lamp. Grasping the pistol tightly, she moved into shadows before the door opened. In the dim light, she recognized Oliver Stover. He peered into the cabin, his eyes flaming when he saw her pressed against the wall.

Reaching for her, he said, "Now we can continue what your big brother interrupted a few months ago."

"Stay away," Becky warned as she lifted the pistol, but Oliver laughed derisively, grabbed her, and pulled her toward him. Becky tried to break his grasp on her arm, and screamed when the gun discharged right beside her head. Oliver staggered backward, and a foolish grin spread over his face. He reached for her again, with life-less hands, before he crumpled to the deck. Blood gushed from the wound in his chest.

Still holding the heavy pistol, Becky hurried to Matt's empty cabin, then staggered to the deck. She saw the river licking the sides of the *Allegheny*. Daylight wasn't far away.

Becky rushed into her cabin and knelt beside Oliver's body, but she turned aside, sickened by what she saw. His breath came in feeble gasps, and she had no doubt that he was dying. Jumping up, she backed into Matt in the doorway.

"What have you done, child?" he demanded, pausing at the threshold.

In broken, breathless phrases, she blurted out the horror of the past few minutes, adding, "Where were you? I knocked on the paneling when I heard him at the door."

"A noise on the main deck awakened me. I heard the shot while I was checking that out."

"Do you think he's dead?" Becky whispered.

Matt knelt beside Oliver. "Not yet, but he can't possibly live with a bullet that size in him." He lifted Oliver into his arms—not an easy task, for Stover was a tall man.

"Clean that blood off the deck. I'll take his body and dump it on one of the side streets. Apparently no one else has heard anything. We'll leave right away."

"Shouldn't we report this?"

"Becky, do you want to hang for murder?"

Her lips trembled, and she said, "It was an accident."

"The Stovers are important people in Gallipolis, and you wouldn't stand a chance of a fair trial. He deserved shooting, so it doesn't bother me that he's dead. Your safety does concern me."

He shouldered his way through the door before she could answer. Becky fidgeted near the gangplank, while she waited for Matt to return, her eyes trying to pierce the foggy atmosphere. She heard footsteps on the brick street, before she saw the shape of a man approaching, and she sank to a bench when she recognized Matt.

"Did anyone see you?"

"Not that I know of," Matt said, and he turned angrily toward his sister, his black eyes snapping. "I hope you're satisfied now, Becky. At last your wanton ways have brought us to this. I have tried to tell you that no good would come of it if you led men to lust after you. Now we have a murder on our hands, and it's up to me to protect you from what you have done."

They had been through similar scenes so many times. No use to argue with him, but she had to try once more.

"I have *not* led any man to lust after me. I barely spoke to Oliver Stover. What can I do about the way I look? God made me this way." Taking a deep breath, she added, "There's one solution to your problem—let me leave you. You won't have to worry about me then."

"Leave me—to do what?"

"Oh, I can go to work somewhere. If you didn't keep me a prisoner on this boat, I might find some man I'd want to marry."

A thoughtful look came into Matt's eyes, and he gazed at her so long that she squirmed. "We can't talk about it now. I'm going to rouse the crew so we can pull out of here."

In less than an hour Gallipolis had been left behind.

Aunt Lizzie had reached the boat just as a deckhand lifted the gangplank. "What in tarnation?" she had growled. "Did he intend to leave me behind?"

Becky stood in the shadows, trying to be as inconspicuous as possible as she stared toward the sleeping town. "He probably didn't know you weren't on board."

Aunt Lizzie's calico skirts had swayed around her worn brown shoes as her slight frame stomped angrily toward the galley.

Stunned, Becky lay on the bunk most of the day, with her eyes closed. When she didn't budge at mealtime, Aunt Lizzie checked on her, walking into the cabin without knocking, feeling Becky's head. "Are you sick?" she demanded.

Becky didn't answer.

"Well, you ain't got no fever, that's for sure. But those freckles on your pale cheeks show up like stars on a cloudless night.

"You and Matt been in a fight?"

When Becky remained noncommital, the old lady stomped out of the room with a snort.

The act she'd committed terrified Becky, but she was more alarmed over her faltering faith.

Over and over she had repeated her favorite Scripture: "Delight thyself also in the Lord; and he shall give thee the desires of thine heart. Commit thy way unto the Lord; trust also in him; and he shall bring it to pass." But the words she had first heard from the itinerant preacher who had opened God's Word to her heart could no longer comfort her. The psalm that had kept her at peace through the years of Matt's domination seemed powerless to console her for the fact that any life beyond the *Allegheny* pointed toward the walls of a prison.

The swiftness with which Matt moved the packet downstream indicated his concern and did nothing to lessen Becky's fears. Every time they moved into a landing, she hid in her cabin, thinking some authorities from Gallipolis would board the boat to arrest her.

One day Matt summoned her to the pilothouse, and announced, "I'm selling the *Allegheny* when we reach Cincinnati; we won't be coming upriver again."

"Why, Matt!"

"We can't travel along this river again. If our part in the crime is suspected, the sheriff will be waiting for us the next time we dock in Gallipolis."

"But if the law wants to find me, we can easily be located in Cincinnati."

"The Stovers have been involved in several shady deals, so I'm hoping that someone else will be blamed for his death, but I'm afraid to risk it. So we won't be in Cincinnati; we're going to Oregon."

Becky listened in stunned disbelief while Matt detailed his plans. "I'll start a steamboat line on the Columbia River," he said. "Oregon isn't even a part of the United States, so Ohio's laws won't reach you out there."

"But Matt, we don't even know Oliver was killed. Why run away without knowing the truth? I'll wonder all my life if I've committed a crime. I won't go."

"I've thought about going to Oregon for a year or so," Matt said, ignoring her comment, "and this may be God's way of getting us out there."

"You have strange ideas about God, Matt, to think He'd have me shoot somebody just to provide you with a reason to go to Oregon."

"Sister, I promised Ma I'd watch out for you, and I can't leave you alone for a minute that some man doesn't force his attentions on you. While we're traveling to Oregon, we're going to say we're husband and wife." Becky gasped and frowned her displeasure, and he added hurriedly, "It's just till we arrive in Oregon."

"Matt Miller, are you crazy? We travel for months with a group of people, pretending to be married, then suddenly at the end of the journey, we'll mention that it was all make-believe! That's probably against the law. We're already in enough trouble."

"Everyone will be aware that we haven't lived together as man and wife. Besides, it's scriptural, Becky. Both Abraham and Isaac claimed their wives were only sisters during difficult periods of their lives. It's the only way."

"Yes, and look at the trouble they got into. I just won't

do it! When are you going to stop treating me like a child?" Her blue eyes sparkled, and she shook her head violently, tumbling the soft, blond hair around her face. "I just won't do it!" she repeated.

"You don't have any choice. Even now, I'm afraid that I can't take you out of the country before you're tried for murder."

"But we don't even know that I murdered anyone!"

Then Becky thought of Oliver's face when he had slumped to the floor of her cabin, and turning her back on Matt, she acquiesced ungraciously. "It's your decision, Brother, and you can take the consequences, but don't think I'm going to tell anyone that you're my husband."

The break with Aunt Lizzie was Becky's most difficult time. Sniffing, she said, "But what are you going to do, Aunt Lizzie? Why don't you come to Oregon with us?"

"I don't have the money to go to Oregon. Right now, I'm going down around Nashville to visit my boy and his family. Don't rightly figure they'll want to see me, thinking I've just come to be a burden on them, but I'm going anyway."

Becky watched a gleam of adventure fill Lizzie's eyes. "T'would be fun though to head out toward the frontier." Becky saw the gleam fade, to be replaced by sadness. "Too late for me, missy." Quickly then, she enveloped Becky in her bony arms. "You're just like my own, Becky. Wish you luck."

While Matt made arrangements to sell the boat, Becky packed their clothes into two small trunks. She couldn't decide what to do with her painting supplies, for Matt had said to take only the essentials, and she was sure her brother wouldn't consider paints and canvases necessary. He'd never paid much heed to her artwork anyway, although she'd lined the galley's walls with scenes she'd painted during their journeys along the Ohio River.

But Mr. Hamilton, the Cincinnati merchant who bought the *Allegheny*, paid attention to them when he came on board with Matt to look over the boat. He peered intently at each painting as he walked around the galley, and he turned to Becky.

"I see you're an artist, miss. Since your brother tells me you're leaving for Oregon, I'd like to make you a proposition."

Matt lifted his head warily, hanging intently on Hamilton's words.

"I own a newspaper here in Cincinnati and am involved in the publishing business besides. I've been looking for someone to do a pictorial history of the West. If I provide you with plenty of supplies, will you keep a log of your journey to Oregon by painting the things you see as you travel along? When you arrive on the West Coast, send the paintings to me, and I'll pay you well for your time. If we print the pictures into a book, you would receive royalties from time to time. What do you say?"

Becky started to look at Matt for his decision, but since she had determined to win her independence from him, she might as well start now. "Yes, I will be pleased to do the paintings."

"Good. If your first volume goes over well, no doubt I can find other commissions for you."

Excitement over her new work lessened the pain of leaving the *Allegheny*, but with Fluff held tightly in her arms, she climbed to the pilothouse for one last look. She didn't know that Matt was already there until she entered. He stood with one hand absentmindedly rubbing the big wheel. Appreciating the sacrifice he was making for her safety, Becky walked close to him and placed one hand over his. He started as if he had only then become aware of her presence, and though his heavy eyelids hid his thoughts, his halting words disclosed his sorrow. "I guess I mind more than I thought I would, Becky. We've had a good life on the river, but there are new opportunities ahead."

Picking up a crate that held the *Allegheny*'s whistle, Matt walked downstairs without a backward glance. The pale winter sun hovered on the horizon, and a few frogs lazily commented on the coming of spring, Becky's favorite season on the Ohio River. She lifted a hand to her aching throat, and a sob escaped her lips as she followed Matt off the boat.

Despite the late spring chill, Becky breathed deeply of the fresh air, savoring the spray from the giant paddle-wheels as it flecked her face. She hadn't realized how much she would miss the *Allegheny* until they had spent some miserable weeks traveling overland from Cincinnati to Saint Louis. But today, when they had boarded this boat to travel to Independence, Becky had the sensation of coming home. Even Fluff seemed happier now that she could hold him in her arms, rather than cooping him up in a crate, as he had been on that stagecoach.

Becky and Matt sat with their backs to the west, watching the sunset's rays of crimson and violet turn the waves from the wheels into glimmering rainbows. Delighted with this natural phenomenon, Becky didn't see the approaching canoe until Matt pointed downstream.

At first the vessel was merely a bobbing speck on the face of the water, but as they watched, it rapidly changed into a rustic canoe containing a single passenger. A crowd of men surged forward to the rail.

"Ho! Who arrives, Indian or white man?" one shouted.

"Must be in a big hurry. Rate he's traveling, he'll overtake us in no time."

"Say!" the other man returned, "that looks like Maurie Davis."

"I've heard of Davis. Used to be a fur trapper, didn't he? Hear he's moving to Oregon for good."

Becky watched as the canoeist disappeared from her sight on the port side of the boat, and she heard a shout, "Here, Davis, throw me your packs."

The buckskin-clad stranger pitched several leather-bound packs to the men; then with a boisterous leap, he grabbed the rail of the packet, and vaulted aboard. The empty canoe bobbed aimlessly on the waves spawned by the paddlewheels.

The passengers crowded around the newcomer, pounding him on the back and shaking his hand. "What happened, Davis? Miss the boat?" one man asked.

"The packet from New Orleans was late. I didn't have time to wait a week for another vessel. I thought I could catch this one if I paddled fast enough," Davis answered, a note of weariness in his soft voice.

"That must have been quite a trip. Come on in the saloon for a drink."

"No drinks for me, but I sure could use some food. Haven't had anything to eat for twelve hours."

With a sweep of his arm, a burly boatman pushed the spectators out of the way. "Lead the way, Davis," he said. "We'll find you something to eat."

Becky peered with interest at the average-height newcomer, who glided silently on moccasin-clad feet as though he normally walked where secrecy and quietness were essential. She saw a clean-shaven man, with black hair neatly trimmed to the base of his neck and eyes so dark that they resembled deep caverns.

Maurie Davis, the men had called him!

The waning light obscured the bench where Becky sat, and Maurie didn't look her way as he passed by, but she didn't miss a move he made. And he was moving to Oregon! Suddenly, for no good reason at all, she regarded the dreaded journey to that territory with a mixture of delight and anticipation.

2

*T*hey stayed in Independence a week before Matt signed on with a caravan.

"I think I've made a good choice, Becky," he told her as they ate their supper in Barker's Boarding House. "This man only takes a small group of wagons and comes well recommended by the merchants. He's had several years' experience in the West as a trapper. He's taking a herd of cattle, aiming to start a ranch in Oregon. Becky, I hate to tell you this. . . ." Matt hesitated, refusing to meet her eyes. "We can't take Fluff," he blurted out, as if eager to rid himself of the bad news.

"Can't take Fluff!" she cried, experiencing a sinking sensation she hadn't known since the day her mother died.

"I'm sorry, Becky." She didn't doubt the truth of that; she'd never seen such a woebegone expression on his face.

"But why? What could Fluff possibly hurt?" Hot tears pricked her eyelids.

"It just happens to be a rule of the trail. He says that dogs cause a lot of trouble, barking and all."

"Then why can't we go with another caravan? Surely some people take their dogs."

"I didn't know about it until I'd already signed up and paid for his services. You'll just have to give Fluff away."

Becky opened her mouth to argue further, but her attention swerved to a man moving among the tables, looking for an empty chair. She recognized him immediately as the man who had so dramatically boarded the boat in mid-river during their trip from Saint Louis. She had thought about him many times during the past week, and at any other time she would have been glad to see him.

Most of the tables were crowded, and Matt indicated the empty chair beside him to the newcomer. Removing his hat, with a slight bow toward Becky, the stranger sat down.

"Becky, this is Maurie Davis, the wagon-train pilot," Matt said, with no explanation about their own relationship.

So this man she'd mooned over was the one who'd banned Fluff! Becky couldn't keep her lips from trembling. "Matt says you won't let me take my dog."

"I'm sorry to make you unhappy, Mrs. Miller." Startled, Becky directed a quick look at Matt, who speared the steak and potatoes on his plate. "Two thousand miles is a long way to take dogs; besides, they bark at the livestock, and if they caused a stampede, some person could be injured."

"But Fluff isn't like that," Becky protested. "He's well trained, and he won't cause any trouble at all. I have a crate for him, and I'll keep him in the wagon out on the trail. He's just a little dog. Let me show him to you."

"Now Becky . . . ," Matt said, but he shrugged his shoulders when Becky rustled toward the stairs. "I'm sorry, Davis," she heard him say, "you came by at the wrong time; I'd just gotten up enough nerve to tell her. Once she turns those blue eyes on you, you'll see why I argued with you about the dog."

Hurrying down the stairs with the white dog in her arms, Becky was glad she'd worn her pink dress with the white ruffles at the neck. Maybe her appearance would make an impact on Maurie Davis.

Becky held Fluff toward Maurie. "See, he's so little that I can carry him most of the time."

Maurie pulled at his collar, as if the shirt had suddenly become too tight, and he seemed to welcome the diversion when the waitress brought his food.

But Becky couldn't finish her meal until she knew Fluff's fate. "Are you going to let Fluff go to Oregon?"

"All right, take him," Maurie said ungraciously, "and I hope I won't be sorry I let you talk me into it."

Smiling, Becky sat down, placing Fluff beside her feet, where he sat quietly, peering eagerly around the room, as if to prove that his conduct would be acceptable.

"I've bought our wagon and other supplies," Matt said to Maurie. "As soon as I buy the mules, we'll be ready to travel."

"Our camp is west of town," Maurie said. "Move out there whenever you like. We won't be starting for a few days."

"I'd like to hire a man to drive my wagon part of the time."

"Usually the women help with the driving," Maurie said, "or do you have more than one wagon?"

"Becky doesn't have to do that kind of work, and I can afford to pay someone to help," Matt replied testily.

Becky flushed as Maurie flashed a skeptical look in her

direction. Matt must have noted it, for he continued, "I figure this trip will be difficult for Becky anyway, without giving her an extra burden of driving a span of mules."

"Oh, Matt, I'd rather drive if the other women do."

"No," he said, and that settled the matter.

Maurie smiled slightly, and Becky knew he'd come to the wrong conclusion about their relationship, but he said evenly, "Since you won't need a driver all the time, why not let one of my men drive your wagon when you want to ride? You can pay part of his wages."

"I don't want a young man," Matt replied bluntly, a comment that earned Becky another appraising glance from Maurie.

"I have two older men who are good drivers."

When Maurie finished his meal and stood to leave, Becky touched his hand lightly. "Thank you, Mr. Davis. I'm not usually such a baby, but Fluff is all I have left of the past. It would have broken my heart to leave him behind."

Maurie moved his hand away from Becky's touch—it might have been a natural gesture, but somehow Becky felt rebuffed.

"Don't mention it, Mrs. Miller; we want our trail companions to be happy."

"Don't leave this room," Matt commanded, giving Becky her orders before he left Independence for a two-day trip to buy the mules for their overland trek. "I've instructed Mrs. Barker to bring up your meals. When I return tomorrow evening, I'll take you downstairs for supper."

Becky didn't comment. "And keep the door locked," he added as he left the room.

Since he hadn't asked her to promise, all morning Becky pondered, *Do I dare disobey him?* She wanted to make some sketches of the local landscape and send a small portfolio of paintings to Mr. Hamilton before they left Independence.

Already she had depicted many of the local scenes that she could observe from her room. An Osage Indian, who paused for an hour opposite the hotel, his dusky face decorated with vermilion paint, and his dark hair bristling with feathers, had come to life beneath her brush.

Becky critically surveyed her sketch of a mountain man, who wore buckskin clothing that he must have made himself, for it was tied together with crude leather thongs. He carried a long muzzle-loading gun, and a powder horn hung at his side.

With her brushes, she had also brought exciting, odorous, dusty Independence to life. Crude hotels and taverns, shops of wheelwrights, wagon makers, and outfitters lined the street through which a yoke of oxen pulled a bright, giant-wheeled wagon overloaded with furniture, plows, animals, women, and children.

Yes, Becky's efforts so far pleased her, but although she had looked intently for the past few days, she had evidently exhausted all art subjects to be seen from the spider-stained window.

While Becky slowly ate the lunch Mrs. Barker brought her, she considered her determination to rid herself of Matt's dominance. *Well, I won't do it by sitting here in this dingy room. It isn't that he doesn't want me to see Independence; he doesn't want Independence to see me.* They had been in the town for ten days, and in that time, she had been out of the hotel for two short evening walks, with Matt always by her side.

For a moment she halted indecisively. Placing Fluff in his crate, she donned a blue chambray bonnet that matched her eyes and dress, picked up her satchel of art supplies, and ventured downstairs.

She hesitated on the wooden steps, looking to right and left, before she stepped boldly out into the dusty road. Staying close to the buildings, she walked westward, careful to avoid the gaze of any man she met. After fifteen minutes, she stopped walking in disappointment. She had come to the end of the street; only open prairie lay before her, and she hadn't observed anything she hadn't already seen from the hotel window.

Looking longingly at the vast area before her, she wanted to go farther, but her newfound independence deserted her. Tufts of new grass pushed upward through the dry stalks of last year's growth, but still the prairie looked barren and lonely. A powerful wind swept across the fields, making it necessary to hold her bonnet in place with one hand, while her eyes sought to penetrate the desolation that lay beyond. At a sound behind her, she whirled quickly, dropping her satchel of painting supplies and spilling the contents on the ground.

A man approached, riding a magnificent sorrel horse. He jumped down, an action that caused Becky to step backward in alarm, but he stooped to pick up the paints and brushes she had dropped.

"Good afternoon, Mrs. Miller."

Blood rushed to her face when she recognized Maurie Davis. She opened her mouth to tell him that Matt was her brother, but halted, not quite daring to risk Matt's anger.

Becky gazed upward, nodding a greeting, before she hastily averted her eyes and reached for the satchel he still held.

"I hope you weren't planning to go any farther by yourself," Maurie commented.

"No, I wanted to find some new scenes to sketch, but I suddenly ran out of town."

"You're an artist?"

"An amateur one, I guess. We had a French artist travel on Matt's boat one summer, and he taught me the basics of painting. I've dabbled around on my own since then. I'm going to make a pictorial history of the Oregon Trail as we journey westward."

Maurie laughed, and she warmed to his carefree manner. "That's a good idea; you'll have plenty of time, and it will relieve the monotony of the trip."

Starting to retrace her steps, Becky said, "I've made a few paintings of life here in Independence, and I had hoped to do some sketches of the local landscape today, but I'll have to forget that, I suppose."

"I don't mean to interfere, but it isn't safe for you to be wandering around by yourself. Couldn't your husband accompany you?"

"*Matt*," she emphasized the name, "isn't here today. He went to buy some mules and won't return until tomorrow."

"I'm going fishing this afternoon in a little creek that would make a good picture, if you want to go along."

Becky glanced quickly at the man, and she had the feeling that he regretted his impulsive words. She lowered her head so that the wide brim of the bonnet hid her face and shuffled her feet in the grass. Was this the type of man Matt warned her about? She thought he was young enough to displease Matt and certainly handsome in a rugged sort of way. But mutiny against her brother surfaced again, and she said, "Is it far to walk?"

"Too far, but I can rent a buggy at the livery stable, and we can be there in no time."

Becky fidgeted, and her pulsebeat raced as her newly

emerged freedom suffered more than one pang of remorse, before Maurie returned in a one-horse buggy. His
manner, when he jumped to the ground and helped her
into the vehicle, was as respectful as anyone could have
desired, and Becky lost some of the diffidence she usually
felt in the presence of men.

In a slow drawl that Becky liked, Maurie explained, "I'm
going to a creek that flows into the Missouri, where the
river changes its southward course and flows due east.
I've caught some good catfish there, and I promised Luke
I'd bring some back for our supper."

"Luke?"

"He's my best friend, who's going with us to Oregon.
Today, he's our cook."

The horse trotted easily over the smooth terrain, and in
a short time Maurie guided him through a low range of
hills into a wooded area, stopping the buggy in a glen
along the bank of a willow-shaded creek. Across the
stream, the grasslands extended westward, but looking
northward through the cottonwood trees that weren't yet
in full foliage, Becky saw the curve of the muddy river as
it surged eastward.

"Will you be able to make some paintings of this?"

"Oh, yes," Becky murmured delightedly as she threw
back the bonnet to dangle over her shoulders. Her blue
eyes gleamed, and the sun streaming through the trees
spotlighted her hair, turning it into shining gold. She
turned a beaming smile upon Maurie, who stared at her
hair, and she wondered at the strange expression upon his
face. He caught his breath and turned away.

"This is a beautiful place, and just what I wanted to
paint. Since we won't have much time, I'll make pencil
sketches now and then do the painting when I'm back at

the boarding house. By using watercolors, I can have them ready before we leave Independence."

"Then I'll leave you here and go upstream to fish. I probably won't wander out of sight, but if I do, I won't be out of hearing, so you call if you need anything."

Sitting on a blanket that Maurie took from the buggy, Becky quickly sketched the placid creek, the seemingly endless prairie beyond it, the wide Missouri River, and several birds that hovered in the trees near her. Standing, to ease her cramped muscles, she glanced upstream.

Maurie had stuck his fishing pole in the bank, and he leaned idly against a tree, waiting for the bobber to sink. Taller than her brother, Maurie was slender where Matt tended toward brawniness. His buckskins clung to him, exhibiting the rippling muscles in his body with every move.

Becky laid aside the sketch pad and pencil, reaching instead for some watercolors. Studying him intently, she portrayed Maurie on the sheet propped in her lap. An occasional breeze ruffled his black hair, and he checked his line a time or two. Once he drew out a fish about a foot long, which he placed on a stringer. But Becky painted his relaxed, confident manner as he leaned against the tree. He seemed to represent the freedom she hoped to find in the West, and her skillful fingers transferred that thought to the paper.

"About finished?" Maurie asked at her side. She hadn't heard his approach, and she tried to hide the portrait, but it wasn't dry enough to put in the satchel.

"Yes, I've sketched a lot, and I guess we should be returning to Independence."

He knelt beside her. "Let's see what you've done."

Timidly, she held out her sketches, and he praised her skill. He looked at his portrait with a strange expression, before he said, "What will you entitle this one? 'Wagon-Train Guide' or something like that?"

The title "Westward We Go Free" had been in Becky's mind, but she hesitated to tell him that. He might consider it a stupid name to give a painting.

They talked very little on the return trip, which ended too soon for Becky, although she was eager to make finished copies of her sketches. She thanked Maurie as he drew up before the rooming house, and as he helped her from the buggy, he said, "It was my pleasure, Mrs. Miller."

"Please don't call me that, call me Becky. And please, don't tell Matt where we went today." She ran up the steps without giving him a chance to answer.

Becky didn't leave her room again until Matt returned the next day, and in that time, she completed the series of drawings that she wanted to send to Mr. Hamilton. While selecting the prints to send, she studied Maurie's portrait for a long time. Then she placed it in the bottom of her box of art paper. Although she thought it was the best painting she'd done, she couldn't part with it.

3

Maurie had set up headquarters along a creek that flowed lazily into the Missouri, and the day before the scheduled departure Matt moved his wagon out to the campsite. Becky counted twenty wagons beside theirs. Eagerly she examined the one that would be her home for the next six months.

Built like a ship, the wagon bed was higher at both ends than it was in the middle, and over the top, eight wooden bows supported a white canvas cover. The steamboat whistle was stored on one side, and Fluff's crate stood near the driver's seat, but everything else consisted of essentials. Labeled bundles were divided evenly on each side of the vehicle, with everything anchored securely to the wagon frame. A narrow passage through the middle was the only unoccupied space, and Becky supposed she would spread her bedroll there.

Matt led Becky to the corral, and looking pleased with himself, he said, "I bought a present for you, Becky. See the little bay mare over there? She's yours. Her name is Beauty."

Becky gasped. "Matt! Do you mean it? Will I be riding a horse to Oregon?"

"Well, you won't be riding all the way, but at least you can alternate between the wagon seat and the horse."

Matt told Becky it was all right for her to walk around while he corralled the mules. "Don't go far away though, for we're supposed to take supper with the Hopkinses. They've got a daughter about your age."

Becky walked timidly among the gathered wagons. Women cooked over open fires, while several men carried supplies to the wagons. One man painted the bottom of his wagon, and sniffing as she passed, Becky decided he must be waterproofing the vehicle, since it smelled like the tar that Matt had often put on the hull of the *Allegheny*.

Memory of the *Allegheny* brought a pang of homesickness to Becky, and seeing a small man bent over a campfire brought Aunt Lizzie to mind. Wondering what her friend was doing now, Becky came face to face with the man as he straightened from his work.

Comprehension came slowly to Becky, but her mouth flew open and she had trouble finding her voice. "Why . . . ," she gasped as the man removed a corncob pipe from his mouth.

"Howdy, young lady. My name is Henry VanMeter. Be you going to Oregon with us?"

Now a person can cut her hair, don men's clothes, and start smoking a pipe, but there was no way to disguise the voice and personality that Becky had known daily for years.

"Aunt Lizzie," Becky squealed, but she lowered her voice when the faded brown eyes flashed a warning.

"What are you doing here dressed up like that?" she whispered.

"Young lady, you've never seen me before. I'm Henry VanMeter, all right." But she gave Becky a sly wink and whispered, "Tell you about it when I get a chance. Don't let on to Matt or anybody."

"But Matt will know you."

"Matt Miller is blind as a bat about some things. I'll keep out of his way. You go on before somebody gets suspicious."

Becky walked on in a daze. For the five years they'd lived on the boat, Lizzie Brannan had been her only friend. Whatever the reason for her presence here, Becky was relieved to know that Lizzie would accompany them to Oregon, but she was puzzled. *Why did Aunt Lizzie have to be so secretive?*

Because she'd had so little companionship for years, that evening Becky enjoyed the Hopkins family. Mr. Hopkins was a preacher, journeying to Oregon as a missionary. Short and fat where her husband was lanky, Mrs. Hopkins soon put Becky at ease with her jolly laugh and pleasant manner. Sixteen-year-old Susie, a smaller edition of her mother, chattered constantly, making supper a genial affair.

Several members of the caravan gathered around the Hopkinses' wagon, and Becky had her first glimpse of Maurie's partner, Luke Brown, a gray-haired man whose cheek bulged with a wad of tobacco. Compared with Maurie, Luke wasn't much to look at, for his clothes hung in disarray over his stooped, wizened frame. Yet as he smiled in a reassuring way Becky decided he would be a good friend to have on this journey.

When most of the emigrants settled down for a talk, Reverend Hopkins asked hesitantly, "Mr. Davis, on the boat coming here, I talked to a man who said that trouble was brewing in Oregon between the American settlers and the British. Are we going to risk our lives and everything we have on this journey, only to find ourselves embroiled in a war in Oregon?"

"I wouldn't worry about it, for I'm not, and I'm risking as much as you are. It's true, the American settlers are tired of this joint occupation with Britain, and they want to become a part of the United States. By the time we reach Oregon, hostilities, if there are any, will probably have ended."

A man standing beside Reverend Hopkins shook his head. "I don't know about that, Davis. On our way here from Missouri some soldiers stopped our wagons and searched them. Seemed to think the British are smuggling arms into Oregon."

"Well, I've been friends with both the American settlers and the Hudson's Bay officials in the territory. I try to live peaceably with all men, so I don't want anyone in my caravan meddling in the conflict in Oregon. If anyone plans to take sides in this dispute, one way or another, he can stay behind."

At that moment Becky glanced at Aunt Lizzie, who stood in the shadows at the corner of her wagon. Her face wrinkled into a wry grin, and she favored Becky with a wink. Becky looked away quickly, fearful Matt might have observed the gesture, but he had glanced in the other direction.

"Since about everyone seems to be here," Reverend Hopkins said, "why don't we take the time to become acquainted?" A tall, homely man, whose lean frame was crowned with a thinning fringe of brown hair, Hopkins looked frail, but his voice sounded deep and resonant.

"There are only three of us. I'm Reverend Alvin Hopkins, and here are my wife, Sarah, and Susie, our youngest daughter. We plan to organize a church among the American settlers in Oregon."

When it came time for Lizzie to speak, she muttered in a voice that Becky couldn't recognize, "My name's Henry VanMeter." Matt didn't even look her way.

Becky wondered what Matt would say about them. He simply commented, "This is Becky, and I'm Matt Miller. I intend to start some kind of river transportation in Oregon."

Next to speak was a young man, slight of build, who sat with an arm around his wife. "I'm planning to turn over some of that rich soil in the Willamette Valley that my cousin, Jason Lee, has been writing about. I'm Jed Cox, and this is my wife, Rose." Her heavy coat didn't hide Rose's pregnancy.

Although Becky listened intently to all the introductions, it was difficult to remember each one. Two young brothers, Bill and Stanley Leviatt, from Illinois, traveled with their mother, a pale-faced woman, who had trouble breathing and had to be assisted by one of her sons when she walked.

Four families had been neighbors in Missouri, and they had planned the trip together. The man who had mentioned having their wagons searched by soldiers was Sam Johnson, whose wife held their only child. Becky counted ten children in the group, but amid the hurried introductions, she couldn't match the youngsters to their parents.

Becky was relieved to learn that none of the people came from Ohio or Pittsburgh, so there seemed little chance that any of them knew her. Before they went to their wagons, Matt brought his part-time helper to meet Becky, although she couldn't imagine why, because the man acted terrified. Dressed in old buckskins, his face was covered with grayish whiskers. He bobbed his head at Becky and moved away without a word. No, she could tell Matt had nothing to fear from Rusty Smith.

Before they went to their wagons, Reverend Hopkins took his Bible and stood before them. "Since this is our last night before departure, let's have a time of worship and ask the Lord's blessings on our journey. Think for a moment on a portion of Scripture from the eleventh chapter of Hebrews: 'By faith Abraham, when he was called to go out into a place which he should after receive for an inheritance, obeyed; and he went out, not knowing whither he went. By faith he sojourned in the land of promise, as in a strange country. . . . ' "

Becky hadn't thought of their pilgrimage as a spiritual one, but she guessed it might be. Reportedly, thousands of Indians lived in the West, few of whom had heard about Christianity. Perhaps these emigrants could be the stimulus for the spread of the Gospel. True, the Whitmans and their fellow workers had already forged ahead in working among the Indians, but surely there was something this group could do.

Better set your own spiritual house in order, before you start a missionary effort with others, Becky's conscience reminded her. Realizing the truth of this thought, Becky heeded the preacher's closing remarks more closely.

"Whatever our reasons for going to Oregon, we must have faith to set out on this unknown road—faith in ourselves, faith in our pilot, faith in each other, faith in God.

"Shall we join together in singing a familiar prayer song?"

A lump rose in Becky's throat, preventing her from singing as the voices of the others rang out:

O God, our help in ages past,
Our hope for years to come. . . .

Be thou our guide while life shall last,
And our eternal home.

Becky's spirit responded to the message of the song, and she breathed a sigh, knowing that her relationship with God had definitely improved since that grisly incident aboard the *Allegheny*. While the others sang she experienced the presence of God.

The emigrants seemed reluctant to leave the campfire, but Maurie recalled them to the rigors of trail life by his words, "We'll have to roll out at dawn in order to leave by seven o'clock. If you expect to eat at the short noon stop, prepare food in the morning. Have your wagons in line when we're ready to roll or be left behind. I'll sound a bugle to arouse you at daybreak."

"Matt," Becky called as soon as she entered her wagon. She sensed something was wrong when she stumbled over a carton in the aisle that hadn't been there when she left the wagon.

Holding a lantern aloft, Matt peered inside to see his neatly wrapped packages strewn in disorder, the bedrolls untied, and barrels overturned. Becky quickly placed Fluff in his crate, which had a broken slat, and stepped outside to join Matt.

But he had run toward Maurie, who strode across the camp circle. "My wagon is a wreck. Looks like a tornado has hit," Matt shouted.

"Yours, too?" Maurie said. "So is ours. Go to the left, Matt, and check with the other emigrants. I'll see what's been disturbed on this side."

In a short time they returned to tally their findings. "So every wagon in this camp was ransacked," Maurie said, "with the exception of the Hopkinses' wagon and the one belonging to that old gent, Henry VanMeter. Of course, those wagons are there side by side, where all of us were gathered."

After working for several hours to reorder the wagons, the emigrants discovered nothing had been taken from anyone.

"So I don't know what to think," Maurie admitted to Matt. "It might have been an effort to delay our departure. No doubt about it, the first wagons across the plains have the best of it."

"But they might have been looking for something they didn't find," Matt reasoned. "I can't seem to get out of my mind what that Missouri farmer said about someone smuggling guns into Oregon."

"I suppose we should be comforted that they didn't find any. Now we know that none of our people are involved in that."

But, Becky thought, *two wagons weren't searched—one belonging to Henry VanMeter, alias Lizzie Brannan.*

"If it was an effort to delay us, someone is going to be disappointed, for sleep or no sleep, we're rolling out in the morning."

That night, Becky wasn't sleepy, and she squirmed on the hard surface until she had the covers twisted and wrinkled. Finally, she sat up, rested her back against some boxes, and reached for Fluff, who was wriggling for attention.

She dreaded the trip to Oregon and wondered if she had the stamina to make it. Because of Matt's protectiveness, Becky had never had the opportunity to prove her mettle, but she suspected that before she reached Oregon she would be put to the test.

Tears came to her eyes, but she wiped them away and determined to be brave. She hadn't been happy on the boat and should be looking forward to a new beginning. Matt had been more congenial since they'd arrived in Independence, so perhaps if she didn't aggravate him on the trail, he might allow her more freedom when they arrived in Oregon.

Becky's pulse quickened as her thoughts turned to Maurie Davis. She had hoped that during the introductions tonight she would learn something about him, but neither Maurie nor Luke had volunteered any information about themselves. When she had questioned Susie, the girl had said, "Maurie told Father that he'd lived out here on the frontier for ten years and that his home before that had been in New Orleans. He's highly recommended as a guide."

Was he married? Becky was convinced that Matt had some reason to believe that his sister had nothing to fear from Maurie Davis. Although Maurie had stirred Becky's interest from the first, she knew she'd have to conceal that fact from Matt. "But how can he become interested in me when he thinks I'm married?" she whispered for Fluff's ears alone, and her anger rose when she remembered how unreasonable her brother could be.

With Fluff still clutched at her side, Becky settled back into bed, with a smile. "It's a long way to Oregon, Fluff, and Matt can't watch me all the time."

When she heard the bugle, Becky jumped from her quilts and dressed hurriedly. A frigid wind had chilled the wagon, so she donned some woolen pants and shirts that Matt had bought for horseback riding and added a cloak and a pair of heavy shoes.

Matt had a fire burning, and in the nippy air she relished the warmth. He handed her a cup of coffee, and she warmed her hands on the tin.

"We'll have some sowbelly and eggs for breakfast, and

I've put some biscuits in that Dutch oven for our food at noon."

"Don't suppose we'll have many more eggs."

"I've packed a few in sand, which will keep them for a few weeks. I noticed one of the Missouri farmers has a crate of hens on his wagon, but I doubt they will produce enough eggs for all of us."

Becky gave Fluff his breakfast and had everything cleaned up when Matt returned with the mules and her horse. All around her people worked in feverish haste.

Despite the early hour, many Independence residents were on hand to watch their departure. Some stared wistfully as Luke, driving the lead wagon, bawled, "Wagons westward! Oregon, here we come."

Becky reined her horse to one side until the wagons passed. Aunt Lizzie was second in line, and she winked at Becky. "Ride with me someday, child, and we'll have us a long talk."

Matt's wagon was pulled by four mules, as were most of the other vehicles, and when he came abreast of her, he cautioned, "Stay close, now!"

Behind him, the elder Hopkinses waved to Becky, and Susie, who looked half asleep, peered through the partially closed canvas. One by one the wagons passed, until Becky was alone on a bluff overlooking Independence and the Missouri River. She stared wistfully at the little town, until Maurie rode up.

"Not wanting to go back already, are you?"

She shook her head. "No, I don't want to stay here, but I don't mind admitting that I'm scared. Still, it's nice to know I'm part of a group heading into the wilderness. I feel the way my ancestors must have felt when they came to America, looking for a new start."

Maurie nodded understandingly. "Americans have felt

the lure of the West since the first English came to Jamestown. The West has always been a magnet to me, but I have a different reaction this morning, when I realize I'm doing this for the last time."

"But you chose to move to Oregon, didn't you?"

"Yes, and I've already filed on land out there." He motioned to a herd of cattle climbing out of the river valley. "That's the beginning of my cattle ranch, if I can get them to Oregon."

"I suppose all of us wonder if we will make it, yet I saw hope mirrored on most of the faces as the wagons passed me; it's as if they were leaving behind memories they wanted to forget."

Maurie stared into the distance, but apparently his eyes didn't see the wooded hills on the other side of the river, for he said bitterly, "Yes, I guess there are certain events all of us would like to forget."

Confused by the sharp timbre of his usually soft voice, Becky thought, *I imagined this man typified the freedom I've come west to find!* Timidly, she dared to question, "You, too?"

Silent a moment longer, he laughed lightly. "Come on, Becky, let's go to Oregon."

He wheeled his horse, galloping toward the head of the line. Becky followed more slowly, watching him. Maurie's soft buckskin shirt hung several inches below his waist, but Becky noted a gun strapped around his middle. A rifle rested in a holster on his saddle, so Becky deduced their pilot would take no chances on this trip.

Becky rode beside Matt's wagon the rest of the morning, but they rarely spoke, except to comment on the landscape. Few trees had taken root on the low hills, covered only with grass so lush and green that the mules kept lowering their heads to nip the tender blades. The piercing song of meadowlarks resounded across the trail, and mag-pies scolded saucily as the wagons disturbed their nesting.

The caravan covered many miles during the morning, and by noon Becky's legs were so numb from the unac-customed riding that when she slid from the saddle she collapsed on the ground. Tenderly, Matt lifted her and carried her to the wagon.

"That was a long ride for you, Becky; I should have thought of that. Rest now, and I'll bring you something to eat."

"Let's walk this afternoon," Becky said to Susie, when the journey resumed after an hour. "My seat feels bruised from that saddle, and my legs are still numb."

Matt tied Beauty to the rear of the wagon, and Becky and Susie trudged beside his wagon, leading Fluff on his leash. The pampered dog didn't like the muddy spots or the strange birds that flew over his head, so he begged to be carried. A brilliant sun dispelled the cold air, and Becky soon removed her heavy coat.

By mid-afternoon, having had enough activity, Becky crawled into the back of the wagon, and despite the jolting vehicle, she slept a little. When Luke finally halted the wagons for the night, Becky proved useless around the campfire. As she watched the other women, who must have been tired also, bustling around taking care of their families, her conscience smote her. *Tomorrow*, she thought, *I'll help with the work, but not now.* She went to sleep with a plate of food in her hands, rousing only when Matt carried her to the wagon.

4

"Matt, how many days have we been traveling?"

Her brother's glance was withering. "Becky, you've asked me that a dozen times today."

"Two weeks, you said, the last time I asked you, so that leaves us twenty-four more weeks to go. I don't think I can take it; admit it, we just aren't cut out to be pioneers."

"Speak for yourself. I'm doing all right. And there's nothing you can do about it. We're committed to this journey, and we have to go on."

The wagon plunged into a small creek bed, mud and water flying as the mules floundered up the opposite bank. The water reminded Becky of one of the ordeals of the trip.

"Do you suppose we'll ever have enough water to wash any clothes?" She held out hands that were grimed from working over the campfire. "I've never been so dirty in my life. No possible way to take a bath. If I try to bathe in the daytime, I'm afraid someone will see me, and I can't see at night. And those new pots and kettles you bought in Independence are so greasy and grimy that I'm surprised the food is edible."

She picked up Fluff from the floor at her feet. "Look at Fluff. I can't believe that only two weeks ago, his hair was as white as snow. Just a dirty gray now. And he doesn't feel good either."

Fluff whimpered a little, and Becky cuddled him close.

"Well, we were crazy to ever start out with that dog. He doesn't have the endurance to stand a trip like this."

Fluff had been a bone of contention between her and Matt right from the first day on the trail. On the *Allegheny*, Becky had washed him often and kept him spotless, in spite of the soot from the boilers. But Matt had been so nasty when he caught her washing Fluff in some water he'd carried from the creek that she hadn't tried it again. She had to be content with brushing him daily.

"And we're never alone," she continued.

"If I remember right, on the *Allegheny* you were always complaining that I wouldn't let you have any company."

"Yes. Now I realize how well off we were. All night I can hear people snoring, coughing, sneezing, and quarreling."

"I'm trying to make the trip as easy as I can for you, Becky, and I might remind you that it's your fault we're still not on the *Allegheny*." Before Becky could retort, he added, "But you let me know when you want to take a bath, and I'll see that no one looks in on you."

They were silent for a long time, and Matt asked, "You've told me all the things you find wrong with this journey—can't you think of anything good?"

Becky thought about his question while they traveled another mile. "Yes, there is some good about it. For one thing, you and I have found a lot of things to talk about, we never talked before. And I've found friends. The Hopkinses are as good to me as they are to Susie, and I like Susie, even though I feel so much older than she.

"I'm actually learning to be helpful around camp. I can travel twelve to fifteen miles a day and still have enough strength to cook our supper. I go to sleep every night without dreaming about that horrible experience with Oliver Stover; in fact, I wish you hadn't brought it up just now."

"I'm sorry, but there's no need for you to worry about the Stovers. We left all that behind."

Becky didn't confide to her brother that Maurie was one of the reasons she liked traveling to Oregon and that his presence eased the vicissitudes of the trail. Every day she found something new to admire about their pilot, and those traits were being transferred to her canvas. For once she'd gotten over the initial fatigue, as soon as they circled for the night she tried to capture on canvas the experiences of the day. Just last night, when she'd checked through her drawings, she noted Maurie was prominent in almost every scene.

Maurie standing knee deep in a stream to assist a wagon. Maurie driving Henry VanMeter's wagon to give the "old man" a chance to stretch his legs. Maurie carrying Mrs. Leviatt to her wagon when she collapsed around the campfire. Maurie standing in his stirrups, waving them westward. In no way could she depict his laugh on canvas, although that was one of his most fetching characteristics—a deep, chuckling sound that they heard often.

Under his influence, she was changing. Yesterday she had seen a butterfly emerging from a cocoon. Watching the creature flexing its wings in an effort to fly, she knew that she was having the same experience. She was alive, where before she had been enclosed in fetters that had bound her spirit. *Westward, we go free,* she thought, knowing her innermost soul had been given a new birth.

"I'm glad we came west, Matt," she said softly, and he favored her with one of his slight smiles.

"I'm going to ride with Maurie to do some scouting this afternoon. Rusty Smith will drive our wagon, but I don't want you to ride with him. Why don't you and Susie walk until I return?"

She merely nodded, thinking swiftly that this was the chance she'd been waiting on to find out what Aunt Lizzie was doing.

After Matt and Maurie departed, she walked with Susie for about an hour, then Susie made it easy for her. "I have a blister on my heel, and I can't walk any more today. Come ride with us, if you want to."

But Becky lagged behind until Aunt Lizzie, who was last in line today, came up with her. She climbed in the wagon.

"Hi, child. I didn't think Matt was ever going to give us a chance to be alone. What's this idea of you two traveling as man and wife?"

"You've got a lot of room to talk about people traveling in disguise. But I'll tell my story first."

She glanced at her friend, who was puffing on a corncob pipe. "I just can't get used to seeing you in those men's clothes and smoking a pipe."

"I've never been so comfortable in my life. Wish I'd thought of this get-up long ago. . . . Go on, what's up with you and Matt?"

How much could she tell without revealing the Stover episode?

"Matt told me he was going to say we were married, to keep other men from bothering me all the time. I had a fit about it, but as far as I know, he's never told anyone that. Everyone apparently assumed that he's my husband. Of course, we never have looked alike."

"You don't even look like yourself now, child. That yellow hair of yours is full of grime; your fair skin is rough and red. But you haven't lost that innocent look from your eyes yet. I always thought that was what drew men to you, more than your looks. You're good-looking all right, if you could get rid of those freckles on your cheekbones and cut down a little on the size of your nose. Has it worked?"

Considering Aunt Lizzie's candid appraisal of her facial characteristics, Becky had lost the chain of thought. "Has what worked?"

"Have the men left you alone?"

"As a matter of fact, they have. Of course, there aren't many single men traveling with us anyway."

"That pilot feller seems like a good catch. Looks like he'd take a second glance at you."

"Well, he hasn't," Becky commented dryly. "But quit evading the subject. What are *you* doing here?"

Animation lightened Lizzie's wrinkled visage. "There's a Bible under the seat. Get it."

Wondering if the old lady had lost her wits, Becky searched until she found the Bible.

"Put your hand on it and swear you'll keep the secret I'm going to tell you."

Not particularly keen to take such an oath, Becky hesitated, but curiosity prompted her. "I swear to keep it a secret."

"Did you ever hear of James K. Polk?"

"Was that someone who traveled on the *Allegheny*?"

"Naw," Aunt Lizzie guffawed. "You know, I told you I was going to Tennessee to see my boy, and while I was traveling down there, I got to thinking I'd like to make this trip to Oregon with you and Matt. I didn't have the money, but I did have a farm down near Nashville that my boy was living on. The land had been given to my man for fighting in the War of Eighteen Twelve, and I let my boy move on it.

"When I got down there to visit, I wasn't treated too well, and I just demanded he pay me for the land, or I would sell it to someone else. He ranted around, but I finally got my money. When word was passed around that I was going to Oregon, I got a message to come and see the ex-governor of Tennessee. That's James K. Polk."

"Well, for goodness' sake!"

"I dolled up a little and went into Nashville, and when I was visiting with the governor, I learned a lot of things I didn't know. Penned up as we were on the *Allegheny*, we didn't learn much about politics."

Becky noticed that they were lagging far behind the other wagons. "Don't you think we'd better move a little faster?"

Lizzie clucked to the mules and tapped them with a whip. "James K. Polk is being considered for Democratic vice-president next time. And just between us, I read ambition in that long, delicate face of his. I think he wants to be president, but howsomever, he told me that the Democrats are going to push annexation of Oregon, if they're elected."

"Annexation of Oregon! You mean take it in as a state?"

"Eventually, I suppose, but it would just be a territory at first."

Becky couldn't think why the idea displeased her, until she realized that Matt was taking her to Oregon to avoid prosecution under United States laws.

"It seems," Lizzie continued, "that the Democrats

wanted someone to take a message about their plans to the American settlers, to encourage them to hold out against the British."

"Do you suppose we're heading into a war?"

"Maybe, but Polk thought if he could send a message to the provisional government to hold out for a few more months, then the United States government would be in a position to deal with the British. Polk says, if the British won't agree to discontinue this joint occupation, the United States will force them to."

"And you're carrying the message!"

"Yep, and that's where you come in. I was told not to reveal my mission to nobody, but, child, I'm almost eighty. I may not make it to Oregon, and I want you to promise me that you'll take the papers on for me if I die."

"Matt won't like it."

"Forget Matt Miller for a while and do a little thinking on your own. He doesn't have to know about it; in fact, he *can't* know about it, for in one of his pigheaded moments, he might tear up the documents."

"Isn't this dangerous?"

"I won't lie to you. It may be. That's one reason I'm traveling as a man. Besides, I doubt if that young pilot would've taken me if he'd known I was a woman.

"Mr. Polk thought there might be some who would try to prevent any messages being carried to American settlers, but I didn't have anything to lose. I'm not going to live long anyway. I suppose I shouldn't involve you, but someone has to be ready to carry on."

"Maybe Maurie would do it."

"I thought of that until that night he told us not to become involved in the political situation in Oregon. I was already involved. What about it? Will you help me?"

"I guess so. . . ."

"None of this *guessing* business. Either you will, or you won't."

When Becky still hesitated, Lizzie said, "Don't you have an adventurous spirit, child? Think of your name being written up in the history books!"

Fired by the old lady's enthusiasm, Becky agreed, but not without one last qualm, "Matt will kill me if he finds out."

"Then be sure he never finds out."

"But I still can't understand why Mr. Polk would choose you—someone he didn't even know, *and a woman*, to carry out such a mission."

"Who said he didn't know me? I knew his family back in North Carolina when Jimmy was just a little tyke. 'Course I hadn't seen him since he was a grown man, but when he heard about me, he knew I could be depended on."

After that first scouting trip with Maurie, Matt often rode with him in the afternoons at the head of the caravan. Not wanting to leave Becky, he allowed her to accompany them. During these rides, Maurie gave them suggestions about handling the horses. Under his tutelage, both Becky and Matt became expert long-distance riders.

Becky was pleased at the growing comradeship between Matt and Maurie, because it gave her an opportunity to be near Maurie quite often without arousing Matt's suspicions. She learned a lot about Maurie through their conversations, which she rarely entered.

Maurie never discussed his youth, but he did describe his days as a trapper. He had been nineteen when he left New Orleans eleven years ago, so he was thirty now.

"I was becoming like the Indians, both worshiping and fearing the elements, but a couple of years ago, I paid a visit to the Whitman mission. After listening to Dr. Whitman a few weeks, I learned that it wasn't nature that should be worshiped, but the Creator God, who had made the world. Whitman introduced me to a new life of faith through God's Son. Of all the experiences I've had on the frontier, that was the most vivid thing that has happened to me, for I was given freedom from some of the problems that had plagued my youth."

If Maurie had continued, Becky might have learned the reason for his reserve toward her, but Matt was more interested in their immediate problems than in Maurie's spiritual condition.

"Some people back in Independence warned we wouldn't be able to take our wagons over the mountains," Matt said.

Maurie considered before he answered, "Some of the vehicles may not make it, for there are places where we'll have to unhitch the wagons and lower them over inclines with ropes and pulleys. Many mountain trails are so narrow that there's hardly room for a wagon to pass, and we'll have to clear rocks to make a road, but wagons have been crossing the mountains the last few years. Most of ours will make it, although I won't guarantee what condition they'll be in when we get there. They may be like Marcus Whitman's on his first trip—after the wagon broke down, he made a cart, but he had to abandon that finally, and they were carrying their possessions by the time they reached the Columbia River."

"Seems as though the roads would be passable by now."

"Each winter, rock slides close the trail," Maurie replied, "making it necessary to clear away rubble in the spring. Since we're the first caravan out, we'll have lots of that to do, but I have some dynamite in one wagon to make our job easier."

"When did the first wagons make it across the mountains?"

"Joe Meek was the first man to take a wagon. Luke and I knew him when all of us were trappers, and when the fur trade dwindled, he decided to settle in Oregon. In 1840, he took his family and several other people through the Rockies in wagons. Meek is an important man in Oregon now; he was chiefly responsible for what happened at Champoeg last summer."

"Champoeg?" Matt apparently had never heard of the place.

"That's where a group of Americans gathered and declared their intention to set up a provisional United States government. Americans make up the majority of the population south of the Columbia River, anyway, and they can see no reason to continue the joint occupation with Great Britain."

As they turned their horses and started back toward the wagons Becky wondered if Joe Meek was the one to whom Aunt Lizzie was supposed to deliver Polk's message. More than once, since she'd pledged her help to Aunt Lizzie, Becky had regretted her impetuous action.

After steady travel for more than three weeks, Maurie called a day's halt at a verdant spot along the Little Blue River. The women especially were happy for a change of schedule, and while the men repaired and greased the wagons, the women bathed, washed clothes, and prepared special foods.

Maurie declared the area north of camp off-limits for the men, and Susie and Becky took a quick swim in the cold water, while Mrs. Hopkins stood guard. Although it was mid-May, the water was cold, so Becky heated enough water to give Fluff a bath and to wash her own hair. For the first time since they had left Independence, she allowed her hair to fall freely over her shoulders.

When she stepped from the wagon, after donning a clean blue dress, Maurie was walking by, and he stopped abruptly, staring at her. She looked at him, her gaze conveying the warmth she always felt in his presence, but he jammed his hands in his pockets and walked swiftly away. Becky gasped at this rebuff, until she reminded herself, *He thinks I'm married to Matt. Would he react differently, if he knew I'm single?*

After a day's rest, the whole group was more relaxed that evening, and they gathered around Maurie's wagon after supper. One of the emigrants, Sam Johnson, asked, "Davis, we've been so lucky on this trip that we can't expect much more smooth going, but can you give us some idea of what's ahead of us?"

Maurie, clothed tonight in new buckskins that revealed every movement of his muscular body, leaned back against his wagon. Unlike most of the men, he was clean-shaven, and he changed his clothes frequently. Luke had on the same pair of buckskins he'd worn when they started from Independence. Glancing around, Becky noted that most of the men were downright unkempt, and she couldn't imagine what they would look like when a few more months passed. Matt had put on a clean shirt and pants this afternoon, but he hadn't shaved since they'd started on the trail. Rusty Smith smelled so rank that Becky couldn't stand downwind of him.

Maurie was plainly trying to encourage the travelers. "It's true that the fastest part of our trip is over, but we'll still have easy traveling until we reach the Platte River. Even there, the road will be smooth enough, but water and fuel are scarce.

"The river's full of quicksand, and only a few crossings

are safe for wagons, but we'll travel on the south side for days before we cross. The water is muddy and full of sediment so we have to carry water with us. The worst to come along the Platte will be the hot winds, and of course, the temperatures will be climbing by then."

"I thought there were Indians out here," Reverend Hopkins queried. "We haven't seen a living soul since we left Independence."

"Plenty of Indians, all right," Luke volunteered, "but they're to the north and west of us. From the time we reach the Platte until we go through South Pass, we'll be in the lands of the Arapaho, the Sioux, and the Pawnee."

"You'll see plenty of Indians around Fort Laramie, Reverend," Maurie offered.

"How far will we have traveled by that time?" Matt asked.

"Fort Laramie is about six hundred miles from Independence. By the way, until we reach the mountains, we won't see many trees, so you women should start picking up buffalo chips for your fires."

Becky recoiled at the suggestion, and revulsion must have shown on the women's faces, for Luke commented, "You'll be surprised what good fires they will make, ladies, and it's a lot easier to pick up the chips than to chop wood. I notice your husbands leave that task to you."

Some of the men grinned sheepishly, for most of them didn't help their wives with the camp chores. Reverend Hopkins helped Sarah, and Matt, too, was an exception. Becky was embarrassed because he wouldn't let her do much, and she knew the other women gossiped about it.

"From Fort Laramie, we continue to South Pass, the easiest approach to the Rocky Mountains. After that, the going is all bad, for the trail worsens, grazing is scarce, and water is limited. Between South Pass and the Columbia, we pass two way stations, Fort Hall and Fort Boise, and we'll all be happy to see them. Trail fever will afflict all of us by then."

Susie, who had been hanging on to every word, said, "Trail fever? What's that?"

"When we're so tired of each other that we quarrel and bicker all the time," Luke commented dryly. "You begin to hate the food, the wagons, the mules, the weather, and each other. We start to think we'll never make it, for every mile becomes harder. Several of us will have died or been killed by then, the animals will be giving out, wagons will be breaking down, and all of you will wonder why you were ever foolish enough to come."

Sam Johnson spoke up bitterly, "You don't paint a very pretty picture for us, Luke!"

Luke nodded wisely. "I didn't intend to."

Maurie smiled, and Becky's spirits, dampened by Luke's speech, lifted a little. "It may not be that bad," he said, "but it's best to be prepared for the worst." He paused, before adding, "That's why I'm pleased you aren't mingling much. When we're stopped for a rest, we can visit, but otherwise, we're better off to stay away from each other."

The next morning Becky discovered red splotches on her arms and legs, and under her clothes were dozens of itching red welts. She saw Luke and asked, "What's wrong with me?"

"Looks like the mosquitoes had a feast on you last night. They're thick along these creek meadows."

"You don't have any bites on you."

"This hide of mine is so tough a mosquito can't bite through it, but your white, tender skin tempts the pests. Surely you had some mosquitoes along the Ohio River."

"Oh, we did, I suppose, but I was never *attacked* by

them before. And," she added, rolling up her sleeve to show him a big welt underneath her arm, "what's this?"

He whistled. "You've got chiggers, too!"

"Chiggers?"

"Yeah, pesky little creatures that poison the skin. They itch like the dickens."

"I know! And I've got them all around my waist."

Luke rummaged in the wagon and brought out a can. "While we're in these low, wet areas, you'd better rub this bear grease on your face and arms. That will keep the mosquitoes away. Put some wet salt on the chiggers."

Becky took one sniff of the can and rejected it.

"Becky, do you want to have mosquito bites, or do you want to stink a little?" She reached out and took the can, saying resignedly, "Give me the bear grease, but no one will come near me."

Later her amused brother only commented, "I can put up with the smell, and if it will keep men away from you, I'd just as soon you used the bear grease from here to Oregon."

5

"So, that's the Platte River!" Matt commented as he momentarily halted the mules.

Rolling hills of sand surrounded the shallow river that must have been a mile wide. Long-legged birds populated the numerous sandbars scattered hit and miss in the riverbed. An island directly in front of them harbored a few windswept, scrawny willows, but no other trees could be seen.

Maurie rode up to their wagon, saying with a laugh, "Think you could operate your steamboat on this stream, Matt?"

Matt merely grunted, but Becky said, "The trees! I miss seeing any trees."

"You won't see many trees for weeks now. The rainfall's just enough to encourage the growth of this tall grass. We'll have good grazing for our animals, but travel along the Platte won't be pleasant for the rest of us."

Susie, returning from a trip to the water's edge, made a face as she passed their wagon.

"Gag! That water tastes terrible, and it's full of sand."

"That's true," Maurie agreed. "You'll have to use the water from the creeks and smaller rivers that flow into the Platte. We'll need to conserve water."

"Conserve water!" Susie answered. "What do you think we've been doing for weeks?"

Nudging his horse forward, Maurie said, "You haven't seen anything yet."

When the wagons turned westward to follow the south bank of the Platte, Becky dropped back to walk beside Aunt Lizzie's wagon, marveling that Matt hadn't yet discovered the old lady's disguise.

"Do you ever wish we were back on the Ohio?"

Aunt Lizzie favored Becky with a compassionate glance. "No, I can't say I do. I kinda like this trail life, though I'm in a bad role. Like to visit a mite more, but don't have a thing to say to the men, and it wouldn't do for me to chin with the women. If it weren't for you, child, I'd be a mite lonesome."

"Why don't you tell everyone you're a woman then? We're too far out for Maurie to make you turn back, and you've proven you can handle your wagon."

"I don't want to make that keen-eyed feller suspicious. I don't like the way he looks at me sometimes, as if he just can't figger me out. He'd be liable to search me, if he knew what I'm carrying." Without drawing a breath, Aunt Lizzie continued, "You're kinda stuck on him, ain't you?"

Becky drew a quick breath. How had Aunt Lizzie learned her secret? She thought she'd been careful.

"Maybe." She paused, glad that Aunt Lizzie had brought up the subject. "But I can't understand his attitude toward me. A few times I've touched him, and he acted repulsed. What would make a man act like that?"

"Course you've got to realize, Becky, that he thinks you're Matt's wife, and any honorable man ain't going to pay you any attention under that condition."

"I've thought of telling him, but Matt and I are getting along so well that I just haven't. I also don't want Maurie to think I'm *inviting* his attention."

With a thoughtful expression on her face, Aunt Lizzie commented, "But I wouldn't be surprised if Maurie ain't been hurt by a woman sometime. He acts friendly and happy when he's with the rest of us, but I've watched him when he's off by himself. At times he's got a bleak look in his black eyes, as if he just can't face his memories. If a woman was back of it, he might intend to keep all women at arm's length."

Travel along the Platte was uneventful for several days, but one morning four of the mules were missing. One of them belonged to Matt. He'd bought some extra mules, so they wouldn't be delayed, but he did want to find out what had happened to the animal. Leaving Rusty Smith to drive the wagon, he and Becky joined Maurie in a search.

"Do you think this is the work of Indians?" Matt asked as they rode eastward, with Maurie studying the ground intently.

"Could be, but I haven't seen any signs of Indians at all. We'll have to start posting more guards and changing them every few hours, so we'll know everyone is alert."

"In this grass, it's hard to track any animals, I guess."

"Yes, especially if they were driven over the route we took yesterday."

After riding for more than an hour without spotting the mules, Maurie said, "We may as well go back; I'll ride ahead this afternoon, maybe I'll find some sign then." Starting to rein in his horse, he stopped abruptly, pointing eastward. "Look at that!"

At first, Becky could see nothing but the tall grass waving in the strong prairie breeze. Then her eyes focused on what had caused Maurie's agitation. Another wagon train was weaving across the prairie.

"Wait here a minute," Maurie said, and he spurred his horse to a little rise above the river, pulling his field glasses from his saddlebags as he rode. He looked at the approaching vehicles a few minutes before he returned.

"I can't believe it," he said as they cantered toward their caravan. "Those wagons aren't more than a day's travel behind us, and I was sure no other group was that near ready to leave Independence when we did. I figured we were more than a week ahead of the main group of travelers."

"We've been moving right along, too," Matt said. "Or at least, *I* thought we'd been making good time."

"We *have* been traveling fast. The more miles we can cover in these early weeks, the better off we'll be when we come to the hard traveling."

"But can it make that much difference? We're still ahead, and that didn't look like too many wagons," Becky said.

"But why are they traveling so fast? Of course, I only counted five wagons, and they could travel faster than we can, especially with my herd of cattle."

"Pretty small group, I'd think. Maybe they want to stay close to us for protection, if they have any trouble."

"*Too* small a group, Matt. No extra animals at all. And the strange thing is four of their wagons are pulled by oxen; only one is pulled by mules." Maurie halted, contemplating. "I suppose you'd recognize the mule you lost?"

"Sure, it's the dumb animal that's been so mean to harness."

"I was thinking it might be wise for us to pay our neighbors a visit." Then, remembering Becky, he shook his head. "But not right now. Let me think about it some more."

"We might be able to sacrifice a few mules to avoid a fight," Matt considered, also glancing at Becky.

Becky knew very well that if she hadn't been along, they'd have gone to the wagons, but she didn't regret her presence. She didn't want either of these two men involved in a conflict that could be avoided.

That night, Maurie detailed guard duty. Three men served in shifts each night, and no more livestock disappeared. He kept the approaching wagons under daily surveillance, reporting to Matt that they apparently weren't trying to close the gap between the two groups.

"You might be right, Matt, that they're a small band that feels safer if they're close to us."

On the nights that Matt pulled guard duty, he asked Susie to sleep in the wagon with Becky. She was pleased to have the girl's company but wondered what her fellow travelers thought. Did they think that Matt didn't trust them or *her*?

After ten days of travel along the Platte, under pleasant weather conditions, one morning, Becky detected a difference in the temperature as soon as she left the wagon. Gray clouds loomed oppressively near the ground; the northwest horizon was obscured; and yesterday's pleasant breeze had been replaced by a cold wind.

By noon a chilling rain swept across the prairie, and the emigrants huddled gratefully in their wagons, for respite from the elements. In a few hours, the wind had increased in velocity, and its arctic bite stunned Becky's face and hands.

With the continuous rain and the wind, the women found it difficult to tend even a tiny blaze. Deciding to share one fire, Becky helped Mrs. Hopkins warm up yesterday's leftover beans; they fried a bit of sowbelly and boiled a pot of coffee. The food didn't stay warm from the fire to their plates, and the strong coffee was all any of them relished. The meal was a silent, miserable affair.

While they were eating, Maurie walked by, and Mrs. Hopkins hailed him. "If we were back home, I'd say we were in for a storm. It feels like snow, Maurie."

Laughing ruefully, Maurie said, "I'm looking for some, ma'am."

"Snow?" Susie shrieked, through chattering teeth. "Why, it must be the end of May!"

"I know, Susie, but weather on this prairie is unpredictable. The season is too far advanced for a blizzard, so we aren't in any actual danger, but it may be mighty uncomfortable. If we have a snow, it will delay us; and that concerns me."

Becky didn't undress before crawling under the quilts that night, but even so, she was cold. The canvas proved no barrier to the whistling, roaring wind that walloped the wagon. She didn't fear that the wagon would overturn, because when they had circled for the night, all of the wagons had been chained together, then anchored to the ground.

Fluff, upset by the wind, whimpered and finally crawled under the covers and nestled against Becky's feet. His added warmth did little to help her feet, and she wished she hadn't removed her boots, but they were wet from sloshing through the icy rain all day, so they wouldn't have been warm either.

She hoped Matt was faring better than she; for the first

time he had erected his tent, and he'd offered to share it with the Leviatt brothers.

Sometime in the night, Becky heard Maurie awakening the men. "Matt, we're having a bad snowstorm, and the mules are drifting with the wind. We need some help to hold them, or we might lose the whole herd."

Matt answered alertly, so Becky doubted that he'd slept either. "We'll be out right away."

Becky pulled back a corner of the canvas, peering at a world that had turned white. Whirling snow prevented her from seeing the wagons on the opposite side of the camp.

When Becky dozed, the wavering wagon catapulted her into dreaming. She was back on the *Allegheny*. Oliver Stover was lying before her, blood oozing from the wound she'd inflicted. She ran from the room, screaming, and she awakened, realizing it wasn't her own screams, but the wind that awakened her. Regardless of the cold, her body was steaming from perspiration, and she buried her face in the covers while Fluff nuzzled her sympathetically.

Would she ever forget it? If Oliver were dead, would he haunt her the rest of her life? No longer sleepy, Becky looked forward to dawn.

When she left the wagon, the snow was still falling, and Matt was scraping away some snow to start a fire. His efforts met with little success, for the light, powdery snow refused to be corralled. Drifts piled high against some wagons, while in other spots the ground was as bare as if it had been swept.

Although they tied a tarp on a frame to shield the fire, breakfast wasn't any more pleasant than their meal the night before. The girls' eyes watered from the smoke, which blew in their faces as they tried to fry corn mush over the flickering fire. No one was surprised when Matt reported that they wouldn't be moving today.

"Maurie says we'll be uncomfortable here, but it's too dangerous to travel and run the risk of becoming separated in the storm." He stayed in camp only long enough to eat, and then he left to spell some of the others who were on guard.

Mrs. Hopkins suggested that they cook for Maurie and his crew, and Becky slyly mentioned, "Why don't we ask Henry VanMeter to eat with us? He can't cook and take care of the stock, too."

Frankly, Becky was worried about Aunt Lizzie, whom she thought was looking more wan every day. How much longer could she manage without help?

Cooking for the extra crew kept all three women busy, and because the snow had covered the buffalo chips, they were reduced to using the fuel they had slung under the wagons for emergencies. About noon Maurie rode into camp, dragging two large dry cedar trees behind his horse; one of these he left for their fire before he took the other to the rest of the women.

Maurie's eyes were bloodshot, his face reddened from the sharp wind. While Mrs. Hopkins cut branches off the trees, to replenish their fire, Susie and Becky rushed around to give him something to eat.

"Thank goodness you found some wood, Maurie," Susie chattered. "We were beginning to wonder what we could do for fuel."

Cheerful as always, he said, "No need to worry about fuel. I brought that fallen tree in from a canyon a few miles south of the trail. There's plenty more if we need them."

Susie poured coffee while Becky piled a tin plate full of venison stew and rice pudding. This was the first time she'd had a chance to do anything for him, and she delighted in such a small service.

Daring to scold him a little, she asked, "Haven't you had any rest at all? You need some sleep."

Between bites, he answered, "I'll rest this afternoon, but I intend to keep close guard again tonight, for I don't want to lose any more mules. The worst is over, so we should be able to move on tomorrow."

"But it's still snowing," Becky objected.

"It isn't snowing much. Most of what you see now is what the wind is whipping around."

Remembering what Aunt Lizzie had conjectured about him, Becky watched Maurie closely as he ate. Has some woman hurt him? So much she didn't know about him; so much she yearned to know.

He looked up to find her watching him, and as their glances caught and held, Becky drew in her breath quickly, for his unguarded eyes revealed his admiration for her. The spell was broken when he lowered his eyes.

"How did you ladies manage through the cold night?"

"I slept fine," Susie chirped immediately. "I've been sleeping on a feather pallet, and last night I wrapped in my quilts and put the feathers over me—slept just like a caterpillar." She nodded toward her friend. "Becky says she was cold."

Warmed now by the knowledge of Maurie's admiring glance, Becky made light of her ordeal. "I wouldn't have been so uncomfortable if I could have kept my feet warm. I was sorry I hadn't slept in my boots, but they were so wet, I didn't want to do that either. If Fluff hadn't slept right beside my feet, they would have frozen." Suddenly she turned around. "Fluff! Where is he? I put him down just long enough to serve your food, and now he's gone." Calling his name, she started a frantic search for the dog.

Wearily Maurie rose to his feet. "Becky, control yourself. He can't be very far away."

"But he's so little; he'll freeze if we don't find him."

At that moment Luke walked into the wagon circle, holding Fluff in the palm of his big, beefy hand. Becky shrieked and grabbed her pet. The shivering and wet dog whimpered pitifully as she hurried to wrap him in a blanket.

"Where'd you find him?" Becky demanded.

"He'd floundered into a snowdrift. As white as he was, if I hadn't heard him crying, he might not have been found. You'd better keep that dog on a leash."

The wind had abated little by evening, and Becky and her friends huddled around the fire. Rose Cox came to cook with them, because Jed was on night duty, and she was lonely. Timid, Rose was only eighteen years old, and she missed her mother, especially since her baby was due in a few weeks.

"What'll I do for help when my time comes?" she whispered. "We didn't think about that when we started out. Jed wanted to come west so badly that I didn't want to delay him on account of the baby."

"Don't worry about that, dear," Mrs. Hopkins encouraged her. "I can help you, and I think Mrs. Johnson, in one of the other wagons, has served as midwife many times. You'll be all right."

By nightfall the camp was clear of snow, because the fires had melted a lot and the brisk wind had blown the rest away. Maurie had warned them to keep the fires to a minimum and to be sure they extinguished them before bedtime. "In this strong wind, stray sparks could easily catch some canvas on fire," he'd explained, and after suffering the effects of the wind all day, no one doubted his word.

Becky dreaded the cold night ahead, but as soon as all the men had been fed, the women doused the fire with snow and sought their wagons. Lifting Fluff into the wagon, Becky realized instantly that something was different in the vehicle. Lying on her pallet was a pair of doeskin moccasins.

"Why, Fluff," she whispered, "where did these come from?" But lifting them to her breast, she knew! No one but Luke or Maurie would have such moccasins, and only Maurie had been told that she couldn't keep her feet warm.

Lost in a bright, little world all her own, Becky forgot the chilling wind buffeting the wagon. The discomfort of freezing weather was nothing compared to the warm, gentle glow that enveloped her body. Hurriedly, she sat on the quilts, removed her boots, and slipped the moccasins on her cold feet. Made from soft, white skin, the footwear was decorated with colorful beads. Although a bit large for her, the moccasins encased her feet in a layer of warmth that matched the flame in her heart. When she wiggled her toes, the beads jingled musically.

Maybe it wasn't as cold as last night, but Becky didn't have any trouble keeping warm. Fluff soon went to sleep, with only his little nose sticking out from the quilts, but Becky lay awake a long time.

After watching the men and their wives along the trail, she wasn't as naive as she'd been when she'd left Independence. She'd often watched Jed Cox and seen the light in his eyes when he looked at his wife. Hadn't she observed that same look in Maurie's eyes today?

How did she feel about him? Her life had been so sheltered that she hadn't talked to other girls about their love affairs, so she had to rely on her own instincts. She wanted to be near him, she liked to hear him talk, and sometimes she had such an overwhelming desire to caress him that it startled her.

Hearing someone walking beside their wagon, Becky peered out to see if Matt was coming in for the night. A man she didn't recognize walked stealthily outside the circled wagons. He passed out of sight behind Aunt Lizzie's, and Becky leaned back and closed her eyes.

How long she lay there, Becky couldn't remember later, but suddenly some inner alarm caused her eyes to pop open. She threw back the covers quickly, startling Fluff into a shrill yip. Peering outside, she saw that a wagon was on fire.

"Fire! Fire!" she screamed. Shedding the moccasins for her boots, she was out of the wagon swiftly, just as Luke jumped out of his wagon and raced toward the burning vehicle. His shot into the air was apparently a signal, for by the time Becky reached the wagon, Maurie was running in from the corral.

"Oh, it's Aunt Lizzie's wagon," she shrieked just as Matt appeared behind her. "Get her out."

Maurie tried to unchain the vehicle from the wagon beside it, and when the chain wouldn't come free because of the frozen snow on it, he drew his gun and shattered the chain with a bullet.

"Luke, throw some water on that canvas. Form a bucket brigade."

Matt was already coming with a bucket of water, a commodity Becky knew was in short supply, since they'd used most of their reserve water during the day. Luke and Maurie started pulling the wagon away from the other circled vehicles, when Henry VanMeter jumped out of the wagon dressed in a nightgown!

"Where'n tarnation you going with my wagon?" Aunt Lizzie sputtered before she saw the flaming canvas, forgetting to disguise her voice. With the empty bucket in his hands, Matt stared at her.

"Aunt Lizzie! What are you doing here?" And he swung on Becky, "Have you known all along who she was?"

Maurie had returned in time to hear this exchange, and he didn't act nearly as surprised as Matt. Had he already deduced that Henry VanMeter was a woman?

The fire was soon extinguished, with little damage except to the canvas.

"We were lucky, that's all. Who left a fire burning?" Maurie demanded.

"Not anyone, Maurie," Reverend Hopkins assured him. "I checked every campfire before I went to bed. No live coals at all."

Becky thought of the man she'd seen right before the fire started, but she didn't want to accuse anyone, so she decided not to say anything before all the others. If they had a firebug among them, no need to alarm the emigrants.

"Well, *Henry VanMeter*, you have some explaining to do," Maurie said sternly.

Aunt Lizzie stood barefooted on the ground, shivering in her flannel nightgown, but she faced Maurie with a defiant look. "Not so much to explain. I'd been with Matt and Becky on their steamboat for years. Just decided I'd like to go to Oregon with them, too."

"Then you're a party to this deception, Matt?"

"No, I'm not!" Matt denied heatedly. "But apparently Becky knew who she was. How come you kept something like that to yourself? An old woman like Aunt Lizzie has no business coming on such a trip!"

"She's made it this far, hasn't she? I can't help it if you're blind to obvious facts. I recognized her the first day in camp at Independence."

Maurie interrupted, "Not much damage to your wagon, except the canvas, and I have a new one you can have, but the wagon bed is wet from the water we threw on it. Can she sleep in your wagon tonight, Becky?"

Throwing her arms around the shrunken, shivering figure, Becky felt the heavy belt around the other woman's waist as she led her toward Matt's wagon. Maurie wasn't going to abandon Aunt Lizzie, but Becky couldn't help wonder what he would do if he knew about the documents Aunt Lizzie carried. *Could the fire have been a deliberate attempt to prevent the delivery of those papers?*

Becky hurried with her dressing, because she sensed some unusual excitement in the camp. Maurie had returned from an early morning inspection of their surroundings.

"Those five wagons passed us in the night, Matt."

"What's their big hurry? I'd like to know."

Maurie shook his head impatiently. "They must have a mighty important reason to be ahead of us to travel as dark as it was last night. Best I can figure, they probably went past while we were fighting that fire."

Maurie took note of Becky, who had joined them. "How's your friend this morning?"

"She won't admit it, but I think she's about done in. I've been worried about her for several days."

"Well, you should never have allowed her to come," Matt said.

"I didn't really think it was any of my business. Besides, she was already signed up to travel when I discovered her. She'd paid her money like the rest of us."

"Naturally, I'd never have agreed to have her with us, if I'd known she was a woman traveling alone," Maurie stated. "But I'm stuck with her now. Today I'll have Rusty

Smith drive for her, if you don't need him, Matt. That will give her a rest."

Luke joined them and took the cup of coffee that Matt held out to him. "I've put a new canvas on that old lady's wagon, and it will be ready to roll with the rest of us. I still can't figure how that fire ignited, unless she dropped her pipe, but the fire started high on the canvas. Don't know what her pipe would have been doing up there."

"I think someone set the fire," Becky said hesitantly. Three sets of eyes turned to her as she hurried on, "I saw a man go behind her wagon right before I discovered the fire."

"Who was it?" Maurie demanded.

"I don't know. I didn't recognize him."

"You mean it wasn't one of our people?" Luke said.

"I'm not sure. It was dark and snowy, and I didn't think much about it, because I don't know all the men in this group very well. But I've thought about it all night, and I do believe the man was a stranger."

Luke and Maurie exchanged glances. "Do you suppose it was an effort to delay us?" Swinging to Matt, Maurie said, "Or could it have been an attempt on the woman herself? Someone who wanted to destroy her. What do you know about her, Matt?"

"She's Lizzie Brannan, and I've known her for several years. She came originally from North Carolina but had lived in Pittsburgh for a long time. Just an ordinary person; I can't believe she'd have any such enemies."

Do I have the right to keep back information that might bring harm to this whole caravan of people? Becky wondered. But she had promised Aunt Lizzie.

"We'll not say anything to the others—no need for everyone to be alarmed." Turning toward their wagon, Maurie continued, "Rouse everyone, Luke; we're leaving here in an hour."

No more snow fell, but the cold wind was penetrating, and all day Becky alternated between the wagon seat and her horse. When they stopped for the night, Luke climbed down from the wagon, sniffed the breeze, and smilingly said, "Chinook!"

Matt, who was near him, queried, "Chinook? What's that?"

"Can't you feel a difference in the air? We're going to get a chinook wind—a warm wind. This snow will be gone by tomorrow night."

The weather was better the next day, and assailed by a warm sun, the snow disappeared almost as quickly as it had come, leaving the grass more luxuriant than before. Deprived of much grazing for the past two days, the mules were determined to stop and nibble the tasty grass, and Matt had a continuous battle to keep them moving.

Anxious to find what lay ahead of them, Maurie rode away as soon as the wagons were on the trail again, and he was gone for two days.

Becky next saw him squatting beside the campfire, tin pan in his hand. He stood up when she came nearer, handing his plate to Luke, who went off to wash it, and clean up for the night.

"Don't let me interrupt your supper."

He hadn't shaved since the snowstorm, and he rubbed his face impatiently, but he smiled, and said, "You didn't. I'd finished."

She looked up at him, and the light in his eyes made it easier for her to ask, "Did you give me the moccasins?"

He nodded. "No more cold feet?"

"Not at all, but I don't suppose I should keep them."

He looked at her sharply. "Why not? Did Matt say anything?"

She gasped. "Oh, I wouldn't dare tell him. I meant, if you'd gotten them for someone else, I shouldn't take them."

He denied this with a shake of his head. "I bought those a few years ago from the Indian woman who makes my buckskins. I only bought them because she needed to get rid of her items before the tribe left the rendezvous. I want you to have them, Becky."

His face was impassive now. Feeling the urge to touch him, Becky lifted her hand toward his face, but her caress was halted when Stanley Leviatt came running across the camp, crying, "Maurie, Ma is awful sick again. Do you have any more of that cough syrup?"

Becky hurried back to her wagon, relieved that Stanley had come in time to prevent her indiscretion.

By morning, Mrs. Leviatt was dead, and the emigrants gathered around the grieving brothers.

"We shouldn't have brought her," Bill was saying when Becky joined the group. "We knew she was sick, but we were determined to have our own way."

Mrs. Hopkins and Eliza Johnson came out of the wagon, apparently having done all that was possible, and Mrs. Hopkins placed her hand on Bill's arm. "Bill, your ma knew her time was about up. The doctor had told her she wouldn't live more than a year, no matter where she was. She wanted to be with you boys when it happened."

"Then we should have stayed to let her die at home, where she could have been buried beside Pa, instead of out here on this dismal prairie."

Reverend Hopkins, who had kept an all-night vigil with the sons, spoke gently, "Her soul has already gone to the

God who gave her life. It doesn't matter where the body lies." Turning toward Maurie, the minister commented, "I suppose we should have the burial this morning."

"Nothing can be gained from waiting," Maurie agreed. "We don't have any lumber to make a coffin; we'll have to wrap her in a blanket." He paused, adding compassionately as Stanley's shoulders shook with sobs, "We should bury her in the middle of the trail and remove all traces of the grave by running the wagons over it; otherwise, marauding Indians or animals might defile the body."

In a few hours, the sober group stood around the open grave, and through her tears, Becky observed the emigrants. No doubt all of them were wondering who would be next.

Stanley and Bill tenderly laid the body of their mother in the grave, and stood with bowed heads as Alvin Hopkins solemnly spoke some comforting words.

Then Mrs. Hopkins started singing, "Jesus, Lover of My Soul." Becky tried to sing with the rest, but the words lodged in her throat. After a final prayer, the mourners watched as Luke and Maurie hurriedly filled the shallow trench. The emigrants offered a few words to the Leviatts. Then everyone stood around helplessly, as though dreading the moment of departure. When Maurie swung into the saddle, all of them drifted back to their wagons.

What else could they do? Becky wondered.

Luke drove the lead wagon across the shallow grave, the others following, but Becky put her face in her hands and sobbed when Matt crossed the grave.

6

Now Becky spent more time with her friend, and Matt had agreed that Aunt Lizzie should eat with them. In return for her help around the campfire, Matt harnessed and fed her mules, a task Aunt Lizzie admitted was more than she had bargained for.

"And I thought life on the *Allegheny* was monotonous, Aunt Lizzie," Becky commented after she had walked for miles in the hot sun, breathing the dust kicked up by the mules. Even at night, when she tried to sleep, the scent of the dust crept in around her.

It must have been almost two endless weeks since Mrs. Leviatt's death. Part of Becky's boredom stemmed from Maurie's frequent absences from the camp, for since they were in the country of the Plains Indians, he spent more and more time scouting.

Riding a short way in front of the caravan, Becky and Susie were the first to see the lone wagon on the prairie before them. Thinking they might be encountering some Plains Indians at last, they raced back to the wagons.

Straining to see what had startled the two girls, Luke said as they approached, "Ho! Looks like we're getting company."

"Indians?" Susie said, having mistaken the wagon for an Indian tepee.

"No, far from it. It must be one of the wagons that passed us back a ways. Go warn the other drivers to keep their guns handy. No telling what might happen. Wish Maurie were here."

Matt pulled his wagon up directly beside Luke's, and they cautiously approached the other vehicle. Becky tied Beauty to the tailgate and climbed up beside Matt.

Luke's gun lay over his knees, but the solitary prairie schooner with the man perched on the seat apparently presented no threat to them. Lifting his hand, he said, "Howdy, I'm glad to see you, neighbors. I had a bit of bad luck; wonder if you could give me a hand."

He motioned toward the rear of his wagon, where an axle had broken, allowing the bed to drop precariously close to the ground.

Luke spat over the side of the wagon, slowly considering the situation. "How come your buddies didn't help you? Weren't you with that small band of wagons that passed us several days back?"

"That's right, and I don't want you to think my friends deserted me. They're in a heap of a hurry, and I insisted that they go on without me; I'd wait for another group of emigrants. I'm not in a big push myself, and I figured there'd be somebody who could help me. My name's Kenneth Hudnall."

Luke secured the reins of his team, shifted his tobacco in his cheek, and climbed down to inspect the damaged wagon. Becky took a good look at the stranger as he walked beside Luke. He had favored her with one appraising glance, and she had immediately looked away, for she didn't like the devil-may-care gleam in his piercing blue eyes above the frowsy reddish-brown beard. Taller than Luke, Hudnall walked with a slight limp while they examined the wagon.

Climbing back up on the wagon seat, Luke said, "We may be able to help you, Hudnall, but not on my say-so. The boss will be in camp tonight, and he'll have to decide. Right now, my job is to get these emigrants settled for the night. We're camping a few miles farther on. Want to ride on in with us, you're welcome."

"It's not too good an idea to leave my wagon alone, is it? Indians might loot it."

"Suit yourself," Luke said as he lifted the reins. "Giddup, mules. Rather lose my wagon than my scalp."

Matt fell into line behind Luke, and as they passed the stranded wagon, Hudnall, sitting on the wagon seat again, lifted his hand in an ironic salute and a mock bow as his eyes met Becky's. Matt said nothing, but a frown marred his visage.

Luke was helping Matt unharness Aunt Lizzie's mules when Maurie rode into camp after a three-day absence. Dust covered his clothes and the prickly growth of whiskers masked his face. He removed his neckerchief and tried to wipe away some of the grime.

"Any problems?" he asked Luke, giving Becky only a brief look.

"Maybe so. Maybe not," Luke said, explaining about the stranger they'd passed an hour before. "I don't know whether or not it's a good idea to help him. Something about it strikes me strange."

"Yeah, it's not likely that the others in his party would

just leave him there. They're at least two days ahead of us. But I don't like to leave anyone stranded. I'll take a look."

Seeing the weariness of his shoulders as he stepped back into the saddle, Becky, with a wary look at Matt, said, "Maurie, if you're hungry, we have some cold biscuits left from breakfast."

The smile he gave her was worth any ire her offer might have provoked in Matt. "Sure would like that, Becky."

She rushed to take two biscuits from the storage box on the wagon bed, cut the biscuits in two, and spread them with honey. She didn't know what emotions were mirrored on her face as she watched him ride away, until she felt Aunt Lizzie's gentle poke in the back.

"Don't press your luck, child. Let Matt see you watching him like that, and you're in trouble."

Darkness had fallen when Maurie returned to camp, with Hudnall following in his wagon, which had been temporarily repaired. Maurie went to Sam Johnson, who had some blacksmith tools, and asked him to fix the wagon.

One of the Missouri farmers agreed to sell a spare axle to Hudnall, and Johnson had the wagon ready to travel the next morning.

"Do you mind if I tag along with you for a few days, Davis? Probably we'll catch up with my friends at one of the river crossings."

"That will be all right, if you follow the same trail rules that we do."

Within a few days, Hudnall had proven himself a problem to the rest of the emigrants. He seemed to delight in arguing religion with Reverend Hopkins; he was constantly whipping his oxen, and the plodding oxen delayed Maurie's caravan, angering Luke. And Hudnall had irritated a Missouri farmer by shaking one of the man's children. Was he deliberately trying to cause dissension among the emigrants?

To Becky's dismay, the man constantly detained her, trying to engage her in conversation. She avoided him when possible, but that wasn't often enough to prevent the black look on Matt's face.

Becky tried to keep Aunt Lizzie or Susie with her all the time, but one evening, while she knelt at the campfire, Hudnall appeared at her side. She glanced quickly around; she was alone. She neither looked at him nor replied to his comments, but when he lingered, she said, "If you know what's good for you, you'll leave before Matt returns."

"Now why should I be afraid of him? Why don't you slip out tonight after dark and take a little walk with me?"

Becky dropped the skillet she was cleaning and jumped to her feet. "I'm not going to stay here and listen to you," but when she started toward the wagon, Hudnall grabbed her by the arm.

"Good! I'll go with you."

Becky jerked her arm out of his grasp just as Maurie and Matt walked around the side of the wagon. Matt uttered a roar of rage, and with one blow to the jaw, Hudnall was spread-eagled on the ground, rubbing his face.

"Get up!" Matt commanded, and when Hudnall remained on the ground, Matt reached for him again.

"Stop him," Becky begged Maurie, who stood by, hand on his holstered gun, with a blazing look in his eyes. "You don't know how violent Matt can be."

But Maurie didn't intervene when Matt took another swing at Hudnall.

"It depends on what he did to you whether or not I stop the fight." The deadly tone of his voice caused Becky to realize that he was as angry as Matt. She was seeing another side to the self-disciplined Maurie—his hand now twitched on the revolver handle, and the look on his face was awesome. Becky recoiled from his anger, but wondered, *If he's indifferent to me, why did he become so disturbed?*

"He didn't do anything to me. I didn't like his company, and I was leaving."

Maurie took Matt's arm. "All right, Matt, leave him alone; let's see what he has to say for himself."

The other emigrants crowded around, and Becky felt her face growing warm.

"I can't see what all the fuss is about," Hudnall said in a surly voice. "Ain't no law agin a man talking to a woman, is there?"

Matt breathed heavily, his face flaming with anger. He started to speak, but Maurie interrupted him. "It seems to me that Miller has the right to resent your manhandling his wife."

Disbelief was mirrored on Hudnall's face as he looked from Matt to Becky. "Wife! I thought she was his sister."

Startled, Becky looked Hudnall over closely. How could he have known that? Had he known them in the East?

"What made you think that, Hudnall?" Matt said, his tone menacing.

He shrugged his shoulders. "That just seemed the way of it. You didn't act like man and wife to me."

Becky sensed dozens of questioning eyes turned first upon her and then toward Matt, as if the emigrants, too, were recalling the strangeness of their relationship.

Not even looking to see how Matt would react, Becky shouted, "I *am* his sister. I've certainly never told anyone otherwise, and I don't think Matt has either. If you've assumed we were man and wife, it wasn't because we lied to you."

Becky met Maurie's eyes briefly, but she didn't look at Matt to see his reaction.

"What next?" Luke exploded into laughter. "Henry

VanMeter turns out to be Aunt Lizzie, and now we have another masquerade revealed."

"Well, I certainly didn't think you acted like Rose and Jed," Susie said, causing a wave of laughter.

But Becky could tell Maurie wasn't amused. "What's the big idea, Matt? I don't recall that you *told* me that Becky was your wife, but you surely didn't try to straighten out the misunderstanding."

Looking sideways at Matt, Becky didn't like the stone-gray cast to his face; he was furious with her.

"If you'd had the trouble I've had for years trying to stop men from forcing their attentions on Becky, you'd realize why I was glad for a little peace on this trip. But since it's been brought out in the open at last," he turned to Hudnall, "I'm serving notice on you, or anyone else who gets any notions about Becky. Wife or sister, Becky is my responsibility, and I don't want her bothered."

"Sorry I caused such a fracas," Hudnall said, but his mealy-mouthed tone convinced Becky he wasn't sorry at all.

Although Becky had expected a tirade from Matt as soon as they were alone, more than a week passed before he chided her about the disclosure. Bone weary from trudging beside the jolting vehicle, she climbed on the wagon seat to rest her feet for a moment. She removed her boots and shook bits of grass and dust from them. Inspecting the soles of the boots, she realized that in a few more days, they would have to be discarded.

Engrossed in considering how many shoes she'd worn out since they left Independence, she'd forgotten Matt's presence, and she jumped, startled, when he spoke.

"Becky, I don't think I can stand Stanley Leviatt one more night, hanging around our campfire, ogling you.

Why on earth you had to tell everyone you were my sister is more than I can understand. We were getting along so well." Matt groaned in distress.

Becky took the scarf from her head and wiped the sweat and grime from her face. "Well, if you think I enjoy his company, you're mistaken. You certainly don't think I've encouraged him, do you?"

Thinking of homely Stanley's face, almost devoid of a chin, atop a long, bony neck with a prominent Adam's apple, Becky couldn't imagine why Matt was jealous of him. But she had to admit that he had become a pest, and last night, Bill had joined his brother. Feeling sorry for them because they'd lost their mother, she had tried to be kind, but she wondered how much longer Matt's patience would hold.

"If you want the truth, I, too, am sorry that I said anything."

Becky didn't know how she had expected Maurie to react when he learned she wasn't married, but if she thought he would join the Leviatts in courting her, she was badly mistaken. He had been gone from camp a great deal of time, and when he was among the emigrants, he had paid little attention to Becky. Piqued at his unconcern, she now wished he didn't know she was unmarried. That way, she would at least have retained her dreams.

But one good thing had come from the revelation she'd made—Hudnall hadn't bothered her anymore. In fact, he was treated as a pariah by the emigrants. His oxen were naturally more sluggish than the mules, and Luke refused to slow his pace to accommodate Hudnall, so he was always last in line, even behind Maurie's cattle. Usually, he was a good hour behind the rest of them.

"Matt," she began, in a tone of voice that made her brother glance at her sharply. "Why are you so possessive with me? It's unnatural for you to try to keep men from courting me. Don't you ever intend to permit me to be married?"

He glanced at her in surprise. "You couldn't have someone here in mind!"

Why, why, why, she pondered, *does he think I wouldn't be interested in Maurie?*

Matt had become more of an enigma to her. His eyes had always been secretive and now, with the heavy growth of whiskers becoming thicker and more tangled every day, he seemed almost like a stranger. His shoulders, crisscrossed by suspenders, were hunched over the reins, and he didn't look her way.

"It isn't that. Maybe I'll never want to be married, but I don't understand your reasoning." Remembering what Aunt Lizzie had once told her, she continued, "Do you know something that I don't?"

Matt chewed his parched, cracked lower lip. He looked straight ahead and seemingly pondered her comment during a full mile of travel, while he flicked flies off the mules, jolted through a buffalo wallow, and hummed a tuneless melody. Finally he sighed wearily, his hands threading his hair, disrupting layers of dust. The rigors of the trail must be extremely difficult for Matt, yet he hadn't complained. Slowly, Becky was beginning to appreciate her brother.

"Yes, Becky," Matt answered, when she had decided he'd forgotten all about her question, "I know something that causes me to protect you, but I'm not going to tell you what it is. In fact, it's been a sorrow to me that I even know it. Wait until we get to Oregon. After we leave this business in Gallipolis behind us, we'll find you a husband."

"Oh, Matt, you're impossible," she mumbled, knowing he'd missed the point completely. "This isn't the Middle

Ages; I have no intention of having you 'arrange' a marriage for me. Before long I'll be twenty-one and my own boss. I'll do what I please then."

Matt didn't seem at all concerned about her threatened rebellion, for he said, "We can ride the horses this afternoon—I've had all the jolting I can take for one day."

They were riding at the head of the caravan to escape the dust when Maurie cantered in from the west. Becky's heart lifted at the sight of him.

Nodding, Maurie said, "There's a small herd of buffalo up ahead, and we'll stop for a couple of days to replenish our meat supply. Do you want to take a look at them now?"

Matt had been looking for some buffalo for days, and he agreed with as much excitement as he ever displayed.

"Is it all right if I come, too?" Becky asked quickly.

"She won't be in any danger, will she?" Matt questioned.

"No, for we won't go close to them. We can look down on the herd from a little knoll, and since the wind is from the west, the animals won't know we're there."

They rode several miles before Maurie slowed down, motioning for caution. Dismounting on a rolling hill, they peered over the edge to a grassy plain where the buffalo grazed.

"What a letdown!" Becky exclaimed. "I don't know what I was expecting, but these creatures are downright ugly. Cattle are much prettier."

About thirty buffalo comprised the herd—rangy animals covered with long, shaggy, brownish-black hair, except on their rumps, where the hair was a lighter brown. Their long necks and bulging humps gave them an awkward look.

But regardless of their appearance, Becky reached for her note pad, which she always carried in her pocket. What a subject for her pictorial journal!

One small calf was grazing by its mother, and she said, "Oh, the little ones are cute."

Maurie grinned at her, seemingly pleased to be sharing her enjoyment. "Just a few cows in this herd, so not very many calves; but there are several young bulls, and they make the best meat."

Matt had been silently observing the animals, and he asked, "Are they difficult to kill?"

"Not with that rifle of yours," Maurie assured him, "but I'll give all of you a few hunting suggestions. Let's return to the wagons, so I can direct Luke to a good camping area a few miles east of here."

Back on the trail, the hot, monotonous landscape made Becky sleepy. The land was flat and unbroken, except for an occasional creek that flowed toward the Platte or by small knolls such as the one they'd climbed to see the buffaloes. The prairie grass was turning brown from the blistering sun, and the dried blades crackled under the hooves of their mounts.

When the evening meal was finished, Maurie sounded a bugle to call the travelers to his wagon. Excitement stirred the group when they heard his news.

After explaining the most accurate way to kill a buffalo, Maurie advised, "I know that all of you are anxious to kill one of the animals, but if everyone shoots a buffalo, much meat will be wasted, for we can't take all of it with us. It will be better to kill only a few and divide the meat among us.

"If we hunt early in the morning, we can have the animals skinned and into camp by noon. Luke will show you how the Indians dry their meat, and we can cure some of

It to take along. We'll save the hides, too. Later on, we may need them to cover the wagons, and when we reach the rocky trails, sometimes we'll tie hides over the mules' hooves for protection."

"What kind of animal should we shoot?" Bill Leviatt asked. "I've heard there's more meat on a cow."

"They have more flesh," Luke answered, "but this time of year their meat is tough and stringy. Besides, they have calves now; if we kill the mothers, we might as well kill them, too. The best ones to shoot are the young bulls."

"I thought there were millions of buffalo out here," Hudnall said.

"Not so many anymore, although we'll see several small herds like this one," Luke responded civilly, without glancing in Hudnall's direction. "One huge herd migrates north in the summer—we may cross that trail before we reach the mountains."

"I'm aimin' to go along, too, Sonny." Aunt Lizzie directed her comment to Maurie. "Have any objections?"

"What do you think you could hit with that old squirrel gun of yours?" Maurie asked with a smile.

"I was shootin' bears with that gun 'fore you were born, young feller. I reckon it can bring down a buffalo."

"If you're going, you'd better ride one of my horses; the mules are too slow."

She nodded, a twinkle in her eyes, and lowered one eyelid in Becky's direction.

The camp was astir with activity long before dawn, and as soon as the hunters were gone, the women took advantage of the two-day stop to cook some of the dishes they'd not had time to prepare during their short evening stops. Rose Cox labored all morning, trying to bake a birthday cake for Jed, although that event had occurred a few days earlier, when she couldn't do any baking.

Mrs. Hopkins stirred up a dried-corn pudding, while Becky prepared beans for baking, and these they buried in the ashes in Dutch ovens. Becky and Susie picked gooseberries for pies, which Mrs. Hopkins soon had baking in their portable stove. With fresh buffalo meat and soda bread, they were looking forward to a sumptuous meal.

After the baking was finished, Becky and Susie bathed in the creek while Mrs. Hopkins stood guard. How invigorating to finally get rid of the bear-grease smell that she'd endured for weeks. Now that her skin had toughened and the rain had ceased, she was no longer afflicted by mosquitoes.

Fluff had a bath, too, and Becky was drying him with a blanket scrap when Luke drove a wagon into camp loaded with three large carcasses. He dumped them on a tarp. "You can start working on these, while I go back for three more."

"Who killed the animals?" Susie demanded.

"Matt, Hudnall, Jed, two of the Missouri farmers, and Aunt Lizzie. Say, that old woman knows how to handle a gun. Wouldn't want to make her mad at me."

"Didn't Maurie kill a buffalo?" Becky asked.

Luke glanced shrewdly at her, but replied matter-of-factly as he climbed into the wagon, "Neither of us were shooting, or we'd have killed some. It's no novelty for us to kill a buffalo—let the others have some fun."

Under Luke's direction, the women cut the meat into thick strips to cure in the sun. "Lay the strips on some canvas, where the sun will dry them, and when we start traveling, tie the meat along the sides of the wagon to finish the curing process."

"Won't the meat get terribly dirty, hanging out that way?" Sarah Hopkins objected.

Luke snorted and said crisply, "The meat will taste good, dirt and all, when we reach areas where game is scarce."

Not doubting his word, the women set to work, and by sunset the meat had been carved and divided equally among the caravan members.

Supper was a relaxed meal, although Becky looked anxiously at Aunt Lizzie, who nodded over her plate. The rigors of the trail were too much for her, and Becky could see that she tired more easily every day.

Becky put worry aside for the moment while she hurried around to help the Hopkins serve the meal. Reverend Hopkins had invited Luke and Maurie to share their food for the evening. Tonight, surely Maurie would notice that she was clothed in a fresh calico dress, and that her hair, clean for the first time in weeks, hung in two heavy braids over her shoulders.

Probably she wasn't as enticing as she had once been, for she'd changed a lot since they'd left Missouri. When she'd bathed in the creek, she'd noted that her body was lean and her skin tough and brown. Although she had thought that washing would restore the luster to her hair, several rinsings had still left it a shade darker than it should have been.

When she'd bemoaned the changes, Sarah Hopkins had said, "Becky, you were only a girl when we started out; you've become a woman now. You seem to have a purpose in life, and it's made a beautiful woman out of you."

As Becky sat with the others, listening to the sound of a fiddle coming from the Leviatts' wagon and the call of a coyote far to the west, she pondered what her purpose in life was. She still believed that God had something for her to do in Oregon. But what was it?

Glancing toward Maurie, she discovered that he was staring at her, his eyes full of yearning, mingled with a pall of despair. Their eyes held for a full minute before Becky lowered her heavy lashes in confusion.

The note was prominently displayed where she couldn't miss seeing it when she opened her eyes. Nailed to one of Matt's crates near the opening of the canvas, Becky reached for it, supposing Matt had left a message for her.

Stretching lazily, Becky tensed when she read the words: THE WICKED FLEE WHEN NO MAN PURSUETH.

Becky's hands trembled, and she gasped for breath.

Staggering from the wagon, she looked frantically for Matt. No one else was astir, and her brother was still rolled in his blankets under the wagon. She knelt beside him, shaking him roughly.

Awake instantly, he took one look at her face in the dawning light and reached out a hand to her. "What is it, child? What's happened?"

She thrust the paper at him. "That was tacked inside the wagon. Who could have put it there and when?"

Matt shook his head, fingers threading through his tangled hair. "You didn't hear anyone around the wagon during the night?"

"No, nothing. Of course, it could have been placed in there yesterday—all of us were away from the wagons, working on the buffalo meat, and it was dark when I went to bed. Oh, Matt, I'm scared."

He patted the hand he held. "I'll take care of you, Sister, the way I always have." He scrutinized the note. Written on the back of a soiled flour sack, it could have come from any emigrant's wagon, for all of them had bought this brand of flour in Independence. The lettering on the note was printed in bold strokes, without a misspelled word, indicating that it had probably been copied from the Bible.

"What are we going to do about it?"

Matt crumpled the paper in his hand as he stood and pulled Becky to her feet. "Nothing we can do about it, I reckon, but keep our mouths shut. Might be somebody's idea of a joke."

"But who knows anything about us? Does Hudnall look familiar to you? Do you think he might have seen us back home?"

"No, I'm sure I've never seen him before we started this journey—or anybody else in this caravan, except Aunt Lizzie. Just forget it, Becky."

But Becky knew she wouldn't forget it, and when the wagons started rolling westward, she eyed all of her fellow travelers questioningly. Someone knew about her past, and she wouldn't feel safe and secure again.

7

*B*ecky hadn't seen the mules more cantankerous, and before the end of the day, Matt, not by nature a patient man, was red in the face, hands shaking in frustration. The mules balked when they came to a slight knoll, and after frequent applications of the whip, they dashed off across the prairie on a run, taking all Matt's strength to control them. Fearing for Becky's safety, he ordered her to ride Beauty and to stay well away from any of the wagons, but even her mild-tempered mount was more skittish than usual.

The other drivers had similar trouble, except Hudnall, whose oxen, looking neither to right nor left, plodded along at their usual pace. Many of the men swore and lashed at the mules, which only made them worse.

Maurie joined Becky, and he looked sympathetically at her, when she asked, "Will we have any worse days than this?"

"I'm afraid so, Becky. We haven't even traveled a third

of the way to Oregon yet. That's the reason it distresses me to see these men abusing their animals—they'd better baby them along. I've tried to tell them, but the stress of the trail makes everyone unreasonable."

"But the mules have certainly been mean today. All the animals have. Fluff even bit me this morning, when I was brushing his hair."

Maurie laughed a little at that. "We're going to have a storm—the animals always sense it first." He pointed westward, where the horizon seemed darker than it had been an hour earlier. "Better have your sketching materials handy—a prairie storm is quite a sight."

By dusk, thunderclouds hovered menacingly above them, and when Becky entered the wagon at bedtime, the depressing heat discouraged sleep. She finally dozed, only to be awakened suddenly by a loud clap of thunder. Sitting up on the pallet, she peered into the night.

Darkness shrouded the camp, and she could barely make out the outline of the nearby Hopkins wagon, but as she watched, her surroundings were lighted by a streak of lightning that zigzagged in a perpendicular streak in the heavens, followed by a bolt that quivered across the sky in multicolored majesty.

A few horses had been hobbled inside the camp circle, and at the next display of lightning they reared, neighing in fright. Thunder sounded in a continual rumble, and after a loud blast that tingled Becky's ears, the heavens must have split apart, for rain poured over the wagon like a waterfall.

A fine spray fell on her face as the rain sifted through the canvas, and as the wind rose in fury, the rain filtered into the openings at each end of the wagon. She attempted to lace the canvas more tightly, but the force of the combined wind and rain moved the wagon back and forth in a rocking motion.

More rain poured through the canvas, and fearing she might be caught in her nightgown if the wagon overturned or the canvas blew off, Becky pulled an already soaked dress over her gown.

Suddenly one side of the canvas gave way. Terrified, Becky pulled on a slicker and jumped to the ground, taking Fluff with her. She didn't know what she was going to do, but she soon encountered Maurie, who sloshed through the rain, a lantern in his hand.

"Becky," he demanded, "what are you doing out in this rain? Climb back in the wagon before you get wet!"

She snapped, "We're already wet; that canvas is leaking like a sieve."

She pulled Fluff from beneath her coat, and Maurie lifted the lantern to look at the dog. With his downy hair plastered to his hide, Fluff looked more like a rat than a dog, and Maurie laughed loudly.

Infuriated, Becky kicked him on the leg. "Don't you dare make fun of Fluff."

Maurie, still laughing, pushed her backward. "And you were talking about the mules being mean!" He picked her up and thrust her inside the prairie schooner. "Stay inside, I tell you; we have to move these wagons to higher ground."

Becky was still seething, and she shouted, "Move the wagons *now*?" Her words were drowned in the fury of the storm.

Bill Leviatt flatly refused to move. Maurie tried to persuade him for a while, but finally he said, "Leviatt, you're moving that wagon. I'm responsible for this group of people, and it's dangerous to stay in this creek bottom."

"It's nothing but a thunderstorm," Bill returned hotly, "and it's only been raining for a half hour."

"I know that, but I don't like the looks of this storm; I think it's raining even harder upstream."

"Then why did you stop here in the first place?"

"Because I didn't know it would rain like this," Maurie answered shortly, his patience obviously wearing thin. "Hitch up right now."

"No, I'm not going anywhere in this storm!"

Bill started back inside the wagon, but Maurie quickly set down the lantern, grabbed Bill by the collar, swung him around, and punched him in the jaw with a force that sent the younger, taller man reeling. Stanley, who had been a silent witness to the argument, grabbed his brother to keep him from falling in the mud.

"Have this wagon ready to roll in fifteen minutes," Maurie commanded as he stalked away.

Coming to stand beside Becky's wagon, Aunt Lizzie cackled, and said, "Looks as if our pilot ain't to be monkeyed with. You'd better not kick him anymore." Looking at her in surprise, Becky wondered if Aunt Lizzie ever missed anything.

In less than an hour, the wagons were again circled on a tableland above the creek. By daylight the rain had stopped, and Matt tried unsuccessfully to start a fire. Becky looked out through the circle of wagons to the creek, amazed to see at least three feet of water where their wagons had been camped a few hours before.

She was watching when Bill Leviatt approached Maurie, saying shamefacedly, "Guess my temper got the best of me last night, Davis. You were right after all, it seems."

Maurie waved aside his apologies. "I just happened to be right this time, Bill. I didn't like the way that stream was rising."

When Bill walked away, Maurie spied Becky and called, "How did Fluff make it through the night, after his bath?" Annoyed, she turned her back and walked away.

Because the supplies had been wrapped in oilcloth, none of them had been damaged. Becky supposed that they would at least stop long enough to dry out their bedding, but the wagons left on schedule.

"We'll never get to Oregon if we stop for a little thing like wet bedding," Luke said as he lifted the reins, shouting, "Wagons, ho!"

Several showers pelted them during the day, and that night they made a soggy, dismal camp not far from the place they intended to cross the South Platte and head northward toward Fort Laramie. Before they left camp the next morning, Maurie returned from a brief reconnoiter, and he called the emigrants around him.

"We have more trouble this morning than we'd expected. These rains have swelled the river where we need to cross. Not many places you can cross this stream."

"Well, can we make it, or can't we?" Luke demanded.

"The mules will have to swim, but the river's still rising, so if we wait any longer, we may be held up for several days." He paused, considering.

"Before we started out, I told you I'd make all the decisions, but I want to take a vote on this crossing. We'll move on down and let you take a look, but I'm advising immediate crossing. For one thing, I've discovered there's another caravan with fifty wagons about a week's travel behind us. I don't know about you, but I'm not hankerin' for that much company."

As the drivers drifted toward their wagons, Maurie continued, "By the way, Hudnall, your friends are waiting on this side of the river. Looks like they tried to take one wagon across, and it sank on them. Probably, you'll want to join them again."

A sardonic expression on his face, Hudnall looked from Maurie to Matt, letting his eyes linger on Becky's face long enough that she sensed Matt's anger.

"Thanks for the kind reminder. I'll do that. Never was one to hang around where I'm not wanted."

The wagons spread out along the banks of the stream, at least a mile wide now, and Becky stared apprehensively at the swirling water.

"But, Davis." Stanley Leviatt voiced the thought uppermost in all their minds, "Do you think we can really cross that stream?"

"Yes, but it can be dangerous. Luke will take his wagon across, while you watch to see how it's done. These wagons were waterproofed before we left Independence, so they will float, and the mules can swim. Two men will ride beside each wagon to help if the mules get panicky. Watch Luke, then make up your minds, and we'll abide by a majority vote."

Maurie gave the signal, and Luke slowly drove his mules to the water's edge. The animals were reluctant to plunge into the muddy stream, and Luke urged them with his whip until the wagon lurched into the water, swaying back and forth for a few moments before it started floating upright.

The wagon swung downstream, but Luke urged the mules forward, while Rusty Smith and another of Maurie's riders eased their horses into the water. Rusty used a pole to prevent the wagon from swinging with the current, and the other man rode beside the mules, pulling on the harness to keep the animals from halting. Slowly, the wagon glided toward the opposite bank.

Becky watched, hand to her throat, hoping the men

would vote to wait until the waters receded. But without much hesitation, the other drivers voted to follow Luke.

Maurie singled out Aunt Lizzie and told her in a voice that left no room for argument, "Rusty will drive your wagon." She looked relieved.

Kenneth Hudnall pulled away from their group and pointed his oxen toward a few wagons about a half mile north. The top of a prairie schooner, weaving back and forth in the swift current, about twenty feet from the bank, was evidence that the Platte River crossing was treacherous.

"Wonder why their wagon sank, Matt," said Becky.

"Could have been a number of things, but all of those wagons look like they're loaded heavily. Probably need to throw away a bunch of things." He strained his eyes toward the other caravan. "Sure would like to know if they have my mule, but guess Davis won't want to start a fight with them."

Becky wished they could go next and have the crossing behind them, but Matt's wagon was tenth in line today, so there was nothing to do but sit and watch. She had ridden down the Ohio on flood waters many times, but she had never liked it, and she dreaded crossing this vast river in a fragile wagon.

Maurie rode across with the second wagon, but before he left, he stopped beside them. "I'll be back in time to cross as you do." He spoke to Matt, but he looked at Becky, as if he had no intention of trusting her to the river without his help.

The wagons continued to cross without incident. When one neared the opposite bank, another vehicle eased into the water. With relief Becky noted that the river was relatively free of debris.

Finally it was their turn, and Becky's heartbeat accelerated when Matt drove to the river's edge. The mules snorted their displeasure, swinging their heads, but Matt held tightly to the reins. Maurie rode on her side of the wagon, and she stared at him with frightened blue eyes. She noticed that his buckskins were wet to the waist and that he had removed his gun and leather bags from the saddle.

"All right, Matt, ease it in," he said calmly, favoring Becky with a reassuring smile, and her hand relaxed slightly on the swerving, creaking wagon bed as it slid into the river. Water splashed into the wagon at her feet, but the vehicle soon righted itself as the mules swam smoothly into the current.

The opposite bank seemed a long way off, but Becky was beginning to be at ease when one of the lead mules started kicking and floundering in the water, swinging the wagon sideways. Matt tugged on the reins, while Bill Leviatt, who was riding downriver of the wagon, tried to lift the mule's head.

"Maurie, take Becky out of here," Matt shouted, and Maurie needed no other invitation. Swinging in close to the wagon, he said, "Don't stand up, Becky, or you might topple the vehicle, but when I lean over, put your arm around my neck, and I'll lift you out."

Becky nodded, but reached back into the wagon, saying, "Wait until I get Fluff."

In his frustration, and fear for her, Matt shouted, "Forget that fool dog, and get out of here before you drown," but Becky had her pet by then and wrapping his leash around her arm, she turned to Maurie.

Standing in the stirrups, he leaned over the wagon, reining his horse away from the swinging vehicle, and when Becky put her arm around his neck, he pulled her easily from the wagon and swung her over the saddle horn.

Becky snuggled close to him and placed her head against his chest while Fluff rode safely between them.

"Matt will make it all right now. Bill has the mule's head above water. They've swept downstream a little, but he's past the swift current."

Right then Becky had no thought for Matt, for with Maurie's strong arm around her, she wasn't worried about anything, and her heart leaped when he put his head down close to hers.

"Are you still scared?" he said softly, hugging her more tightly than the situation warranted, Becky thought.

She shook her head against his chest, lifting her eyes to meet his dark ones. "Not now. I haven't been frightened since you lifted me from the wagon."

"Precious little Becky. No wonder Matt is such a fool about you."

When his horse waded from the water, he lowered her to the ground, and they watched Matt guide his cargo to safety.

Matt's face was red with anger, and he muttered, "It was a sorry day for me when I stopped piloting a steamboat to drive a span of mules." He jumped from the wagon, grabbed his rifle, and aimed it at the offending mule.

Sensing his intent, Maurie grabbed his arm. "Stop it, Matt. Come to your senses; you'll need that mule before we reach Oregon."

"But he might have caused Becky to drown." Turning to her, he said, "As for you, if you ever act so foolish over that dog again, I'll shoot him, too."

Becky gasped, and Maurie said, "Over my dead body you will."

Matt bristled at his words, but Luke stepped between the two men. "You're both crazy! Say anything more, and you'll be sorry tomorrow. No harm done, and we have some more wagons to bring across before dark."

Becky turned her back and walked away from Matt, clutching Fluff close, but Matt caught her arm. Her brother had never found it easy to apologize, but his face mirrored his remorse.

"I'm sorry, Becky; you know I wouldn't hurt Fluff."

"I know that," Becky said wearily, "but Matt, please stop treating me like a child."

Reverend Hopkins's was the last wagon to cross, and when he drew the mules to level ground, he threw back his head and shouted, "Let the people praise Thee, O God; let all the people praise Thee."

Becky raised her voice in exalted shout with the others, and looking around for Maurie, she saw him at the edge of the water, his head bowed in prayer. Becky had even more to be thankful for than the others, now that Hudnall had been left on the other side of the stream.

Luke led the wagons a few miles north of the river before stopping for the night, and at mealtime, Maurie shouted to the emigrants, "Tomorrow we'll start a two-day trek over a waterless tableland into Ash Hollow. We'll spend a few days there, for it's a wooded area with plenty of timber to repair our wagons, and the best water anywhere along the trail. I'm telling you that so you'll have something to look forward to. The next two days are going to be rough."

"I notice you didn't tell the way we go down into Ash Hollow," Luke said quietly, with a mirthless laugh, when the emigrants started drifting back to their wagons.

"Time enough to learn that," Maurie answered as he turned to Matt, who had lingered.

No reference was made to their heated words a few

hours earlier. "Maurie, did you take a close look at those wagons on the other side of the river?"

"Not close enough. When I went to the river early this morning, I thought it wouldn't hurt to be friendly, so I headed toward them, but a couple of men rode out and intercepted me quite a ways from the wagons. I had looked them over with the glasses before I ventured down into the valley—odd, I didn't see any women at all."

"I don't suppose you'd know if those mules they have belong to us."

"No, I wasn't close enough to be sure, and although I'm not normally one to dodge a fight, as long as we can keep ahead of them, I'll call it even."

"Seemed to me as if their wagons were heavily loaded."

Luke said quickly, "What are you thinking, Matt?"

"I just wonder what they have to hide and why Hudnall joined himself to our group. And I keep wondering about those guns that are being smuggled into Oregon."

Maurie smiled slightly. "I've had the same thought, Matt, but I don't know what we can do about it."

"How about coming over to the wagon tonight to give us an idea of what this political situation is in Oregon? If I'm running into trouble, I'd like to know what it is."

At least an hour of daylight was left when Luke and Maurie sauntered over to join them.

"All right, what's on your mind, Matt? What do you want to know about Oregon?"

"Mainly, what's all this fuss between the British and Americans?"

"Several nations have laid claim to the Oregon country, with the United States and Britain being the main contenders. Oregon's boundaries have never been clearly fixed; *Oregon* is a vague name for all the territory west of the Rockies and between the northern boundary of California, and the southern edge of Russian-held Alaska, around the fifty-fourth parallel. In eighteen eighteen, United States officials proposed that a boundary be set at the forty-ninth parallel, but the British demanded a line farther south. Since neither side was willing to compromise, the two countries agreed on joint occupancy."

"If that has worked since eighteen eighteen, why all the ruckus now?"

"Until recently, Matt," Luke said, "the British pretty much controlled the area, for the few Americans out there were trappers, with a few missionaries scattered here and there. But when the missionaries began to write back East, praising the wealth of Oregon, the influx of settlers started."

"That's when the British became alarmed?" Reverend Hopkins asked.

"That's when the British became alarmed," Maurie repeated. "They have several well-armed forts around the area, and many people are loyal to them, but the American settlers resent the Union Jack flying over their homes. A few more years of immigration will swamp Oregon with settlers. The British are wise enough to know that any group of people willing to spend six months of trail life to reach Oregon won't be easily scared away. They're preparing to fight to keep us out."

"Will the Americans fight back?"

"Luke and I were out there last summer during the organization of Oregon's provisional government. Admittedly, that government was started with a majority of only one vote among the citizens living south of the Columbia River, but before we left in early autumn, the settlers had already drawn up a bill of rights and a constitution."

"They'd also started a consistent method of settling the

land," Luke interjected. "You'll have to reckon with those new laws when you stake out your claims."

"Do you know what the rules are, Luke?" Reverend Hopkins asked.

"They're reasonable, I think. Any man can claim six hundred forty acres as long as he builds a cabin within six months. Maurie and I staked our claims before we started eastward, and we threw up crude cabins to meet the rule before we left."

"Do you think the British will actually declare war on the settlers?" Matt said, more interested in the war than land claims.

"I'm hoping the British will decide that these Americans will be an advantage to them as a market for their goods, rather than a threat to their fur trade, which is about shot in Oregon now anyway. But with a few hotheads in Washington and London, we could end up in a war."

"Young feller, do you happen to know the name of the head of that there provisional government you're talking about?" Aunt Lizzie asked, and startled, Becky looked sharply at her.

"George Abernethy was when we left. They'd more or less set up headquarters at Abernethy's store in Oregon City, near the falls of the Willamette River."

Darkness had descended, and Becky stirred the fire into a slight blaze. She liked to see Maurie's face when he talked.

"For my money, I'd bet the settlers will have more trouble from the Indians than from the British. The redskins are growing restless, suspicious of the Americans."

"But surely by now the missionaries have made an impact on the Indians?" Sarah Hopkins said.

"No impact at all, ma'am," Luke said courteously.

"How can you say that, Luke? I've read accounts of

their successes in eastern newspapers," Reverend Hopkins differed with him.

"I haven't read any newspapers, but I've seen with my own eyes. Without the missionaries, the settlement of Oregon would have been delayed for years. But the missionaries haven't changed the Indians."

"Now, Luke," Maurie said, "you know that many of the Indian children have attended the mission schools. It isn't all bad."

"Sure, a few of them have come; I'll admit that, but when they return to the tribes, they revert to their own language, their tribal customs, their old religion."

"You mean the Indians have a religion?" Susie asked, wide-eyed.

"Sure they do. They're more conscious of an afterlife than most of us, and they prepare for it in their own way."

Becky started crying when she looked down into Ash Hollow—tears of joy over the first trees they'd seen for weeks and tears of frustration when she pondered how the wagons could ever go down such a steep hill.

The past two days along the desert tableland had been the worst of the trip. The cattle bellowed for water all during the night, and mules actually perished for lack of water. One of Matt's mules keeled over when they'd stopped for nooning on the second day, and efforts to revive it proved useless. That left only two extra mules, and he had thought he had plenty of animals when they'd left Independence!

"There it is, folks—Ash Hollow—and you'll admit it's worth the trip, but taking wagons down this hill isn't easy," Maurie was saying.

"Surely, Davis, there was an easier way to get here," Sam Johnson protested.

"Some wagons skip Ash Hollow and follow the river, but we save several days by coming this way, as well as having the advantage of making repairs to our wagons and resting ourselves in such a pleasant place."

"Well, how do we get down there?" Matt asked.

"Ladies and animals walk. We'll lower the wagons on ropes. I brought an extra supply of new ropes, for we don't want any of the wagons to break loose."

"It's good-bye wagons, if they do, so be careful," Luke cautioned.

"We'll handle one wagon at a time. Chain the wheels to the wagon boxes, then we'll lower them slowly on our ropes. That will come tomorrow. Tonight we'll take the animals down for water and make camp. We'll sleep on the ground, so take what you need."

Picking their way over the rough, cactus-strewn ground, which punished their sore feet, now encased in broken shoes, Becky and Susie assisted Aunt Lizzie on the steep descent. Reaching the creek in less than an hour, the women fell on their knees and buried their faces in the cool, refreshing water.

Before she took a drink, Becky carried a dipper of water to Aunt Lizzie, who had dropped in the shade of a tree. "I don't think I'm going to make it, child," she said in a weak, quavering voice.

"Of course you are," Becky said with a confidence she didn't feel. "All of us are tired now; for the past two days I've wondered if I'd make it myself."

"Well, if I don't, you know what you'll have to do."

"Yes, I know, and I don't want to think about it. You rest up while we're here in Ash Hollow. I don't want anything to happen to you."

As thirsty as she was, Becky paused to pick a pink prairie rose and to listen to the song of a wren, echoing from the sandy caves behind her. What a beautiful place to rest!

"Doesn't seem possible we've been here three days and that tomorrow we're heading west again," Becky said to Matt, who was completing some repairs to Aunt Lizzie's wagon. Becky was sketching Matt at work, when she saw Maurie sauntering their way.

"Still busy?" he said. "I thought you'd be finished by now."

Matt merely grunted; he'd had all the company he wanted, after most of the children had stopped by to see what Becky was painting and after a double dose of the Leviatt brothers.

Dipping her brushes in water, Becky asked, "Have you been here often?"

"Not so many times, but I saw this area when I came west the first time in eighteen thirty-four; I've never forgotten it."

Crawling from the wagon, Matt said, "You must not have been very old then."

Maurie stretched his legs and propped his arms under his head. He was wearing a brown woolen shirt, just a shade lighter than his hair, and Becky thought she'd never seen a more appealing sight.

"Twenty years old, but lots of boys were younger than that when they took to the fur trade. That was a great life, Matt, and I loved it, but if Luke hadn't taken me under his wing, I doubt I'd have lived long. Many didn't make it through the first year."

"When did you meet Luke?"

"I met him in Saint Louis just a few days after I arrived there from New Orleans. I was looking around for a job, and he found me. It's been a good association for both of us."

Maurie seemed to be in a reminiscing mood, and Becky didn't want to destroy that, but she dared to ask, "Then New Orleans is your home?"

"Yes, I was born there. My father was from Tennessee, and he went with Andy Jackson to fight the British in eighteen fourteen. He met my mother, a French Creole, and stayed there. I don't remember my father, for he died when I was just a baby."

"Your mother?"

"She died before I left New Orleans ten years ago. I had an uncle living in the family home until last year, when he passed away. That's why I went back to New Orleans this past winter. I sold the family home, packed up a lot of the furnishings, made arrangements to have them shipped around the Horn, and completely cut my ties with the East."

"Do you mean you don't have any relatives living in New Orleans now?" Matt's question surprised Becky, for he wasn't one to pry into a person's past.

"Not any of my mother's people anyway," Maurie said easily and sat up, "but that's enough talk about me. I came to show you some things here in the hollow that I thought Becky might like to paint. It's a little late, but I've been right busy since we came."

Picking up the grease bucket tied to the back of the wagon, Matt said, "I'm not going to have time, for I still have to grease our wagon. But I don't suppose there's any reason why you can't go, Becky, if you want to." He gave her a warning look. "Don't be gone very long."

Becky refrained from looking at Maurie, for she didn't want him to see her amazement, but she put her boxes in the wagon and pocketed a sketch pad and pencil. Smiling at each other like conspirators, Maurie and Becky walked away, aware that this was the first time they'd been alone since she'd revealed her true relationship with Matt.

Climbing the steep slopes, Maurie reached out a hand to help Becky, and glancing backward, noting that they were out of sight of Matt's wagon, she left her hand in his. Entering a large-mouthed cave, Maurie pointed at several massive bones of prehistoric animals protruding from the earth.

"I don't know much about ancient history," he said, "but I have heard of the mammoths and mastodons that used to inhabit the earth. These must be remains from that time."

Becky knelt in the dirt to get a better view of a jawbone with giant teeth attached. "What a find! I'm sure this is the type of thing Mr. Hamilton wanted. I've done paintings of the flowers, the birds, the trees here in Ash Hollow, to show what the area is like *now*, but how interesting to see this from thousands of years ago. I'll hurry!"

Maurie lounged beside her, silently watching as she covered several pages with sketches. When she finished and stood to leave, she murmured, "Thanks, Maurie. You've been such a help to me on this whole trip."

"I've not helped you as much as you have me. You've taught me to *feel* again," he said, lifting one of her heavy braids to his lips. "So Matt isn't your husband."

"No, and I'm angry at him for allowing people to think so. He has some strange ideas at times."

Maurie's nearness brought Becky a sense of contentment, and she realized that her happiness was tied inseparably to the man beside her. The light in the cave was waning, and the deep shadows prevented her from seeing his face very well. She moved her hand caressingly along the side of his face, bringing it to rest on his shoulder, feeling the muscles of his arm go rigid under her hand.

His right arm drew her close, and he kissed her lips, gently at first, then with a fierceness that sent little musical chimes coursing through her body. His left arm moved gently over her shoulders and back. Becky returned his kiss instinctively, buoyed upward on the wings of love.

Placing her arms around him, she felt his body tense, and he pushed her away, turning his back on her. He reached out a hand to touch the wall of the cave for support, and she could see he was trembling.

"Why, Maurie, what did I do wrong?" she whispered, wounded deeply.

"It's not *you*, Becky, it's *me*. I thought the wounds of the past had healed, but apparently they haven't. Come on; I'll take you back to Matt." His face ashen-gray, he motioned her out of the cave.

8

Maurie had gone long before the caravan started the next morning, and frustrated and miserable, Becky awaited his return. In addition to her mental anxiety, the heat had intensified. Under the cloudless sky, however, the atmosphere was clear, and the pointed spire of Chimney Rock loomed in the distance.

The mules suffered from the heat, and to spare them, Becky rarely rode on the wagon, electing instead to walk and carry a lifeless and miserable Fluff. Along the rough trail, all day they passed strange rock formations, bursting like volcanoes from the earth. The ground burned her feet through her heavy-soled shoes.

What's the matter with Maurie? she asked herself, still troubled over his unusual behavior in the cave at Ash Hollow. What had Aunt Lizzie said about him, "I wouldn't be surprised if some woman's hurt him sometime"? That would account for it, but why should she have to pay for what some other woman had done?

About two hours before sundown, Luke circled the wagons near Chimney Rock, and Becky gazed at the tall, jagged, needlelike spire pointing, majestically, toward the sky. She would have liked to climb the rocky base, but the heat had sapped what little energy she had. She contented herself instead with making a colorful painting of the noted landmark while Susie hung over her shoulder and watched.

About dark, Maurie rode hurriedly into camp, and he called the emigrants to his wagon.

"I caught sight of a party of Sioux this afternoon, and I followed them until they saw me. They chased me for a ways, shooting at me. I lost them an hour or so ago, but we'll need to post a double guard tonight. These Indians have changed since last year. They seemed more hostile, and they have lots of guns. Fortunately, they don't know how to use them, but they could be lucky and score a hit."

An expectant hush affected the group at once, for Indian trouble had worried them from the first. Becky had never heard the camp so quiet as the emigrants prepared their food and hurried into their wagons. The night passed without incident, however, and with watchful eyes the travelers prepared for the next day's journey.

Before Luke gave his, "Wagons, ho," Sam Johnson asked, "What do we watch for, Davis? This Indian fighting is new to most of us."

"Watch for smoke signals, horses on the horizon, or an unusual movement of any kind."

"Keep these mules moving today," Luke said. "I'm going to set a rapid pace. We can make it to Fort Laramie in a week if we step along, and I aim to."

"How many days have we been on the trail now? I've lost count," Aunt Lizzie said.

"Fifty-five days, by my calculations," Luke replied.

In a half hour, Luke bawled, "Wagons, ho," and the caravan rolled westward. Maurie rode a continuous circuit around the wagons during the day, but Becky noted he avoided their wagon completely. A tenseness pervaded the whole group. But the day passed without any sight of the Sioux, and Becky shared the others' relief when Luke finally gave the signal to halt for the night.

"We still can't relax our vigil," Maurie told them. "I want a constant patrol around this camp tonight. We'll make a rope corral for the livestock, as close to the wagons as possible, but even then we could have trouble, for the Indians can slither through the grass without being seen. And don't any of you wander away from camp."

Shaken by the possibility of an attack, Becky remained wakeful. Without undressing, she lay down on her pallet and pulled Fluff to her side. An unusual quietness settled over the camp, but occasionally Becky heard the hoot of a bird. Or was it a bird? Could Indians be making the noises?

Becky turned from side to side; never before had she realized how hard her bed really was. Not wanting to awaken Fluff, she slipped out of the wagon.

Reverend Hopkins stood guard between his wagon and Matt's, and she went to his side, drawing a shawl over her head as protection from the brisk breeze.

"Is everything all right?" she whispered.

"I don't know," Hopkins answered. "Too many birds around, I think."

"Sounds like owls we used to hear back home."

Becky peered intently into the dark night, seeking out any danger that lurked there. Matt was on duty, but she would feel safer if he were here.

The light started in a small spot, suddenly spreading out like a fan in front of them.

"Fire!" Reverend Hopkins shouted, and a blaze, fed by the wind, spread rapidly through the nearby grass.

Maurie jumped over the tongue of a wagon and into the circle. "Don't panic," he shouted, "it's a trick. Use wet blankets to keep any sparks from setting the wagons on fire. We're going to set a backfire." He ran toward the corral. "Don't leave the animals, no matter what. They're after the mules."

Becky heard the mules braying and the horses squealing in fright. Soaking a blanket in the water barrel, she stood by their wagon to douse stray sparks.

Beyond the wagons, she saw a second line of fire streaking across the prairie grass and the figures of men running back and forth along the line. Once Becky had seen an artist's interpretation of hell, and she was reminded of that now. In the intense heat, people screamed, and the terrified animals went berserk.

For hours the emigrants fought to protect their property, and as dawn beamed slowly across the prairie, they heard the Indians' horses galloping away. Becky watched her fellow travelers assess their losses. Several wagon covers were badly burned, a few of Maurie's cattle had been killed, but the people themselves had sustained no injuries except for minor burns and bruises.

The rope corral had remained intact, and the Indians had not taken any livestock, but the terrified animals still strained against the ropes. One mule, more frenzied than the others, had been roped, but he tugged for his freedom. Finally, breaking loose from Bill Leviatt, the mule jumped over a wagon tongue and into the circle.

"Take cover," Luke shouted. "We may have to shoot the crazy fool."

Becky crawled under the Hopkinses' wagon with Susie,

but she screamed when she saw a white ball catapult from Matt's wagon into the path of the runaway mule.

"Fluff!" she screamed, and unmindful of her own safety, Becky scampered toward her pet. She was conscious of a shot, and realized that someone had shot the mule, but too late for her dog Fluff's hair was mottled with blood. One blow from the mule's hoof was all it had taken to end the dog's life.

Becky was stunned, and only vaguely did she realize that Susie and Matt were kneeling beside her.

"Oh, Becky," Matt said, "don't cry. He didn't hurt; it happened so quickly."

But Becky wasn't crying. She felt as if her face had been turned to stone.

Susie was sobbing on her shoulder, but Becky stared straight ahead, clutching the dog tightly.

"Let me have him, Becky. I'll bury him for you," Matt said, and Becky relinquished the limp body. Tears streamed from Matt's eyes, drenching his unruly whiskers. He and Susie shed the tears for Fluff that Becky could not.

Becky still knelt in the center of the circle, staring into space. Susie brought a strip of blanket from their wagon and carefully wrapped Fluff in it. Matt, periodically wiping his eyes on his shirtsleeve, carefully made a small box out of some scrap lumber.

Maurie apparently had been following the departing Indians and hadn't witnessed the tragedy, for he came into the camp as Matt and Susie, burdened with the box and shovel, walked away. He came to Becky and lifted her to her feet, hiding her face on his shoulder.

"Oh, my dear," he whispered, "I'm so sorry. Is there anything I can do?"

She shook her head. "I want to go inside the wagon. I can't bear to watch them."

She stayed inside the wagon the rest of that day and the next, only coming out to sit on the wagon seat to take a look at Scott's Bluff as they passed by. She didn't want to eat, didn't want to communicate, and above all, she didn't want to think. Fluff had been her only comfort for so many years.

At last, drained of emotion, Becky knew she had to put the past behind her, and the day after they passed Scott's Bluff, she rose on schedule to start her usual activities. Her arms felt empty as she walked beside the wagon, but she tried to concentrate on the long journey still ahead.

"Wonder what we'll find at Fort Laramie, Matt?" she asked, and he looked at her, brightening.

"Not much. It's only a trapper's trading post. There will be a few supplies we can buy, if you think we need anything."

Susie joined them then, asking, "Do you know several of the children are sick?"

"What ails them?" Matt asked.

"They're throwing up, and running off into the bushes most of the time. And a high fever makes them lifeless."

A tremor of fear moved Becky. "You don't suppose it's cholera, do you?"

"Luke doesn't think so. He says they probably got hold of some bad water at our last camp. He told them not to drink any of the water without boiling it, but the children apparently did."

Becky caught an apprehensive expression on Matt's face. "Matt, did you drink some of that water?"

"Yes, I did, as a matter of fact. I didn't have time to boil water."

With a few hours of daylight left after they stopped,

Becky once more left the camp chores up to Matt while she tacked a piece of paper on the wagon bed, so that she could record her impressions of Scott's Bluff. But her fingers refused to do her bidding; having a will of their own, they started sketching Fluff.

Soon the dainty, snow-white dwarf came to life before her. His dark, snappy eyes contrasted beautifully to his long, silky hair. Intelligence, beauty, and amiability were mirrored in vivid detail on his tiny face. And as she painted, the tears that she had harbored inside began to flow, and Becky felt a release of her sorrow.

Seeing what she was doing, Matt patted her awkwardly on the arm. His touch was burning.

"Matt, do you feel all right?" She looked at him closely and laid a hand on his forehead. "Why, you've got a fever!"

He shook off her concern. "Nothing much. I've had a headache all day; it's this hot sun."

But the next morning she heard Matt vomiting before she left the wagon, and by the time they arrived at Fort Laramie, he was slumped on the seat, face twisted in agony from stomach cramps.

Becky hurried to Maurie's wagon, where he and Luke were settling for the night.

"Matt is really sick. Could you come see about him?"

"He's not the only one. Hardly a kid in the caravan that's not sick, several of the women, as well as Rusty Smith," Luke grumbled as he walked along. "And I wanted to leave this fort in a hurry."

"Maybe it's just as well to have them be sick here, in case we need help," Maurie said.

"Well, I've been lookin' for Rose Cox to have her baby anytime, but I hadn't reckoned on this."

Matt was trying to unharness the mules, stumbling

blindly as he went from one to the other, but Luke shoved him aside.

"Here, I'll take care of them."

Matt didn't protest, but sank weakly to the ground, leaning against a wagon wheel. "I can't possibly drive again tomorrow if I feel the way I do now. What a day!"

"I wasn't planning to leave tomorrow—wanted to spend a day at the fort," Maurie assured him, "but with so many people sick, we may have to delay even longer."

Becky had already looked over the fort—a large log structure surrounded by a wall of sun-dried bricks. The barren countryside around the fort was cluttered with many Indian tepees.

"I suppose the Indians come in here to trade," Matt said weakly.

"Yes, but not usually so many." Maurie sounded worried.

The next morning, Matt was still too weak to venture away from the wagon, but he allowed Becky to enter the fort with the Hopkins family. She wanted to paint the fort at close range.

But she couldn't very well put her first impressions on canvas. The fort stank. Horses and burros wandered aimlessly within the walls; Indian men and women lounged in front of the cabins; scrawny dogs fought over food littered on the dirt floor; and half-cured buffalo hides emitted an odor that caused Becky to hold her nose.

Inside the store, the emigrants looked at the few items for sale and wandered back into the courtyard. No one wanted to spend scarce money for coffee beans that cost a dollar for two cups or for flour at fifteen dollars a hundredweight.

With Susie giggling nearby, however, Becky did bargain through sign language with an Indian woman beside the wall and finally ended up with a pair of beaded moccasins. They were not as soft as the ones Maurie had given her, but she could wear these around camp and save her precious shoe leather. The Indian didn't want any money; instead she coveted the faded blue shawl around Becky's shoulders. Not sure she was making a good trade, Becky at last took the moccasins and left her shawl.

Arriving back in camp, the first person Becky saw was Kenneth Hudnall.

"Greetings, Miss Becky," he said, sweeping his grimy hat off and taking a low bow before her.

Seeing Matt's grimace, she nodded and went in the wagon. Hearing his loud laugh, she knew Hudnall delighted in pestering her.

"How'd he get here?" she asked Matt after Hudnall left. Matt was lying on his blanket, and he pointed westward, where four wagons were moving steadily beyond the fort.

"He's outrider for his wagon train today, and he came over to say hello. Or so he said, but I don't trust that bird's motives."

Maurie had been watching the progress of the wagons, and he hunkered down beside Matt.

"Passed us again. Can't believe that they wouldn't even stop at the fort. They're going to have to rest those oxen sometime. Looked to me as if they'd about used up all their strength."

"All except the last yoke," Matt said.

"What do you mean?" Maurie asked.

"That last wagon was moving along easily. The oxen weren't straining at all. Maybe they've left part of their load along the way."

"Well, that happens lots of times. Last year, between here and Oregon, we saw furniture of all kinds lying along the trail. The strongest animals are struggling to pull the wagons by the time they get to South Pass, and people try to ease the load."

"I didn't exactly have furniture in mind," Matt said.

A sudden light broke over Maurie's face. "Guns! Why didn't I think of that? Do you suppose they're scattering these guns among the Indians and encouraging them to attack the wagon trains this summer?"

" 'Twouldn't surprise me. That's the way the British operated in the Northwest Territory for a long time."

"Well, I'm going to take a look in those wagons, one way or another; maybe we can catch up with them at Independence Rock." He looked keenly at Matt. "Think you'll be able to travel in the morning?"

"Sure," Matt said, but Maurie looked doubtful.

"I'm planning to leave, even though we'll be short of drivers. Rusty is still laid up, can't ride or drive. One of the Missouri farmers is sick, but his wife says she can drive the wagon. So we'll leave at the regular time in the morning."

Is Matt sick again? Becky raised on her elbow and peered out through the canvas. Leaning against the side of the wagon, Matt was heaving and gasping for breath. Pulling a blanket around her shoulders, she went to Matt, but Reverend Hopkins was already there, his arm around Matt's shoulders, lowering him to his pallet of quilts beside the wagon.

"Try to take some of this medicine, Matt. Sarah says it will help settle the stomach."

Obediently, Matt swallowed the spoonful of medicine, but he vomited it out on the ground. *Is Matt going to die?* The very thought caused cold goosebumps to break out on Becky's body. *What would I do if he died?*

She'd never seen Matt flat on his back before. He was

always healthy and steady as the sun. The thought of his death stunned her.

Perhaps sensing her state of mind, Reverend Hopkins led her out of Matt's hearing and said, "Becky, you have to get hold of yourself."

"But what if he dies?"

"I doubt that he will, but you have to be prepared. You've put your trust in Matt, when you should have been trusting God. Matt is human, like the rest of us. God is the able one. Remember the Psalmist's words: 'God is our refuge and strength, a very present help in trouble.' "

That was all very well for Reverend Hopkins to say, Becky thought peevishly—his brother wasn't sick.

Matt was still living by morning, still determined to drive his wagon. Stumbling under the load of the harness, he finally succeeded, with the help of Stanley Leviatt, in harnessing his mules, but when he tried to climb on the wagon seat, he collapsed. Becky stifled a scream and ran to him. He was still breathing, so she supposed he had only fainted.

Luke and Maurie came running, and groggily Matt sat up, only to fall back again.

"You'll just have to go on without us, Maurie. We'll wait until the next emigrants come along and travel with them. I can't make it today."

Becky gasped at his statement. Wait here to travel with another group of strangers while Maurie moved westward without her? Wait here, and if Matt should die, she'd be all alone at this fort!

Maurie must have sensed her apprehension, for he said, "We'll do nothing of the kind. You're leaving with us. If there isn't anyone else available, I'll drive your wagon myself. Maybe there's someone at the fort we can hire. Luke, help me lift him into the wagon."

Matt suffered their help without protest, and they soon had him settled on Becky's bed. Remembering Reverend Hopkins's words the night before, Becky prayed, "God, we need Your help right now."

Glancing across the circle, Becky saw the wife of the sick Missouri farmer sitting on the wagon seat, ready to drive out as soon as Luke gave his "wagons, ho!"

Does God always send help, or does He sometimes give people the courage to help themselves? Becky wondered.

Becky was perched on the wagon seat, reins in her hand when Maurie spied her.

"What do you think you're doing?" he demanded.

"I'm going to drive this wagon today."

Behind her, Matt groaned, "Becky!"

"Now you be quiet, Matt Miller. I want you to lie back there and get well. If you think you're going to bring me out here and die on me, you've got another think coming. I'm going to drive this wagon until you're better, so if you don't want me to drive, recuperate in a hurry."

She turned to Maurie, who was standing below her, hat pushed back on his head. "You're holding up Luke. I'm ready to go."

"Becky, you cannot drive that wagon. You don't know anything about handling mules."

"How do you know I don't? If that woman over there can drive, so can I."

Maurie shook his head. "She has worked all of her life. Matt has made a household pet out of you."

Becky's eyes glittered ominously, and Maurie stepped back, no doubt remembering when she'd kicked him once before. His shoulder was on a level with her feet.

"Maurie Davis, I've had enough bossing from you and

Matt Miller, too. I was twenty-one years old just last week, and I'm my own boss. Now step aside."

Maurie turned on his heel. "Don't expect any help from me, when you have trouble," he spat over his shoulder. "Let's go," he said to Luke.

Becky wasn't nearly as confident as she pretended, and her hands trembled on the reins. Luke's wagon moved out, then three others before it was her turn. She shook the lines as she'd watched Matt do hundreds of times and said in a strong voice, "Giddup!"

Nothing happened. Holding the reins in her right hand, she tried to maneuver the whip across the backs of the mules with her left. She grazed the back of the first mule to her right, and he shook his ears a bit, and flicked his tail as if he were bothered by a fly, but he remained immobile.

She laid down the reins, grabbed the whip with both hands, and brought it down across the backs of the two mules to her left. The rear one brayed loudly, bucked in the harness, kicked the mule to his right, and with a snap, all four animals broke into a run. Becky grabbed the seat to keep from tumbling out of the wagon. Dropping the whip, she reached frantically for the reins and caught them just before they slipped out of the vehicle.

Behind her, she heard Matt praying, "God in heaven, help us."

"Yes, help us, God," she added. Remembering that God might expect her to help herself, she pulled on the reins with all her strength, shouting, "Whoa, mules. Whoa, mules! Haw! Gee!" and every other command the drivers used, but the mules continued to run.

She whizzed past Aunt Lizzie's wagon, and the old lady stood up, clapped her hands, and cheered. "Atta girl. Take those mules to Oregon."

Out across the prairie the mules sped, the wagon bed

creaking at every seam. When she passed Luke's wagon, his mouth flew open, and his wad of tobacco tumbled to the ground. Becky still held to the reins, pulling with all of her might, but she had no control over the mules.

A horse raced by her, and with a gasp of relief she saw that it was Maurie. He leaned over and caught the bridle of one of the lead animals. Becky felt their speed slacken. The animals finally stopped just short of a little creek that flowed toward the Platte. They were more than a mile from the rest of the wagons.

"Becky," he began, and fire smoldered in his eyes.

"I'm going to drive these mules today," she said doggedly.

He groaned in desperation. "But you *can't* drive the mules; can't you see that?"

"Now that they know who's boss, we'll get along all right."

"That's the trouble. They *do* know who's boss, and it isn't *you*."

"I'm going to drive these mules today," Becky repeated.

"Do you want to kill yourself—and Matt, too?"

"I'm going to drive these mules today!" Her little spurt of courage was disappearing in a hurry, and Becky had to hang on to that single idea.

Accepting defeat ungraciously, Maurie muttered, "See if you can turn them around and drive back to the rest of the wagons."

He still held the bridle, and with his help, the mules docilely returned to their place in line, where they seemed inclined to walk normally.

When the wagons started again after nooning, Susie had asked her mother, "Why don't I ride with Becky and help her?"

Hurriedly, but subtly, Mrs. Hopkins squelched the idea.

"I don't believe you should, Daughter. The mules have to carry Matt and Becky, too. No use adding your weight to their burden."

Becky understood her reasoning all too well. Mrs. Hopkins would expose her daughter to the dangers of Indian attacks and other horrors of the trail, but not to Becky's driving.

Maurie hadn't spoken to Becky since their heated words of the morning, but she did take comfort from the fact that he didn't stray far from her wagon all day.

Will Luke never stop for the night? Becky's feet were numb from keeping them in one position for hours; her arms felt as though they'd been pulled from the sockets, and her eyes ached from the strain of staring forward all day. *Oh, to lie down and rest,* she thought, but once they stopped, the mules would have to be unhitched, watered, fed, and corralled for the night. Trying to figure out how Matt took off the harness helped Becky forget her physical miseries.

When Luke started circling the wagons, she had it almost figured out. She climbed stiffly over the wheel, holding to it a moment until some circulation returned to her legs. *I'll tackle this mean one first,* she thought, still not having forgiven the animal for causing the runaway. But he might not have forgiven her for whacking him with that whip either, she reasoned, so she started with the mule in front.

Unhook the reins from the bridle, lay back the collar, unhook the belly band. . . .

"I'll take care of that, Becky," Maurie said gruffly, coming to stand beside her.

She ignored him. *Unfasten the crupper, lift the harness off the animal, and lay it to one side.* But Becky hadn't reckoned with the heaviness of the harness, and when she pulled its full weight toward her, she stumbled, caught her feet in the leather, and fell backward under the mule. She felt the wind off the mule's hoof as it went by her.

With a jerk, Maurie pulled her away from the skittish mule. Untangling her from the leather and chains, he drew her roughly to her feet and shook her until her head spun.

"I've had enough, Becky! Do you know that mule didn't miss your head by a hair? Stubbornness can be carried too far. Now get out of here and let me unhitch these mules."

Matt peered out of the wagon with a white face. "Becky, what's gotten into you?" But his eyes narrowed when he looked at Maurie. "Don't you ever lay a hand on her again, Davis! She can do what she wants to do."

"And I intend to drive the mules until Matt is well again."

At that moment, all Becky wanted to do was lie down and rest, but she determinedly helped Aunt Lizzie prepare food, carried Matt his portion, and put up the tent. As soon as she possibly could, Becky crawled in the tent and stretched out. Well, she'd always wanted to be independent of Matt, and she'd proven her independence today.

Independence had its price, though, and she would have traded her freedom for muscles and hands that didn't ache and burn. Thinking of the peaceful life on the *Allegheny*, she muttered, "Why, oh, why did Matt ever decide to take such a trip anyway?"

"Becky," the quiet whisper awakened her.

When the word was repeated, she recognized Maurie's voice, and she pushed back the tent flap.

"Will you come out for a minute?"

Wondering if Matt had heard, she didn't answer, but quietly scooted out of the tent. He took her hand and led her away from the wagons to sit on a large rock.

"What time is it?" she asked.

"About midnight, I think. I haven't been asleep—kept thinking how I'd talked to you today. Couldn't keep my mind off it. I'm sorry, Becky. My only excuse is that I was scared something would happen to you."

"You'd be sorry about that?"

Maurie's arms encircled her shoulders, and her hands moved around his neck. Whatever had ailed Maurie in the cave at Ash Hollow didn't seem to affect him now, for he lowered his lips to hers, kissing not only her lips, but her ears and throat. Then his lips slithered down her arm to the tips of her fingers, which tingled with delight at his caress.

Nudging her ear with his nose, Maurie whispered, "Thank you, Becky."

Almost beyond words, Becky responded weakly, "Thank me, for what?"

"For bringing me to life again. It's been a long time since I've felt clean, felt like a whole person. You've brought me back to myself." He ran his hands through her hair, and said, "I want you to know that I love you, Becky. I can't ever promise you anything more than that, but just to love you has given me a contentment I haven't possessed for a long time."

While she puzzled over his strange comment, he added, "Do you forgive me for how I've treated you today?"

She nodded and snuggled in his arms. "Well, you were right, of course. I didn't have any business trying to handle those mules, but I couldn't see any other way. I was terrified we'd have to stay at Fort Laramie by ourselves."

"I wouldn't have left you there; you should know that."

"It doesn't matter now. Matt is better, and he should be able to take over soon."

Maurie's kisses lingered on her lips long after he'd taken her back to the tent.

The next morning, the mules were less hostile, accepting her commands and her untrained hands. Yet Becky broke camp with a worried mind, for another sign had appeared on their wagon. This time, tacked on the outside, for all to see, was a flour sack emblazoned with the words BE SURE YOUR SINS WILL FIND YOU OUT. Becky thought she destroyed it before anyone else saw, but the question remained, *Who placed it there?* When they stopped for the evening, she still didn't have an answer.

9

When Matt was able to drive, in three days, Becky was more than ready to admit she'd had enough of the mules. It was more pleasant to walk again and chat with her brother.

"I'm really worried about Aunt Lizzie," she told him. "When I think how tired I've been after driving all day, I don't know how she can make it at her age. And she looks bad, too."

"I know that, but I don't know what we can do about it. She made the decision to come along, and she's too proud to admit she needs any help. As far as that's concerned, no one is able to help her much. Everyone wants to rest, but according to Maurie we dare not waste a minute; we have to keep moving along."

Becky tried to take her mind off of Aunt Lizzie by looking toward Independence Rock, which they should reach by late afternoon.

"Are you going to write your name on the rock, Matt? Luke says almost everyone does."

"Nope. In the first place, I don't feel like climbing up there. I'm not too keen on advertising that we've traveled this way, but I suppose you want to paint your name."

"Oh, not particularly, but I do intend to look over the rock. Luke says Kit Carson's name is there, as well as a lot of other famous mountain men."

The sprawling landmark was reached by late afternoon, and Mrs. Hopkins volunteered to cook the evening meal, if Becky and Susie wanted to inspect the huge granite formation. Becky supposed that they shouldn't waste their scarce shoe leather, but she needed some diversion from the incessant plodding along the trail.

Carrying a container of paint and a brush, the two girls walked the half mile from the wagons to the base of the rock.

"Stay on this side of the rock," Maurie had cautioned. Becky knew that he'd be watching for any danger.

After climbing to a small shelf, Becky looked for other signatures, while Susie signed her name.

"I do believe here's Narcissa Whitman's name, Susie. And this could be Eliza Spalding's, too, but it's rather blurred. I heard Luke say that people refer to this as the 'Register of the Trail,' and he must be right. Just think, you'll have your name near someone's as famous as Narcissa Whitman. I hope we can see her when we arrive in Oregon."

Susie stood back to look at her handiwork, and Becky exclaimed, "For goodness sake, be careful; I thought you were going to tumble down the side."

"Here's a funny name. Did you ever hear of Galley Opolis or something like that?" Susie asked.

Becky felt the color draining from her face, and scampered hurriedly to where Susie was examining a signature.

The word *Gallipolis* had been carved with a chisel, and without doubt quite recently, for some of the rock chips were still lying near the inscription. A symbol of some sort was also evident, and Susie peered at it more closely.

"Why, look, that's a hangman's noose! Isn't that funny?"

"Yes, very funny," but Becky's voice shook, and Susie looked at her quickly.

"What's wrong, Becky? You're white as a sheet. Can't you stand heights? Maybe we'd better climb down."

"That's a good idea," Becky said, actually sick to her stomach over their discovery. She stumbled back across the field, paying no attention to Susie's chatter.

Back at camp, she drew Matt away from the others, conscious that Maurie was watching her intently. If she looked as bad as Susie suggested, no doubt everyone could sense her agitation.

Matt certainly did. "Becky, what is it?"

"Someone has recently carved the name *Gallipolis* up there, with a hangman's noose beside it. Matt, is someone following us? If the authorities *are* after me, why not accost me and put me under arrest, rather than engaging in this harassment? What are we going to do?"

Becky had never seen Matt's eyes so bleak and helpless. "I don't know whether I can climb over that rock or not, but I'd better go take a look. I've asked myself your questions dozens of times. I still believe Hudnall is responsible for these warnings, for they always seem to appear when he's around."

Matt returned in an hour, and he agreed that the words had been carved recently, but who could have done the deed, he didn't know.

"Becky, I want you to be careful. I don't want you out of my sight unless you're with Luke or Maurie. I'm sure they wouldn't have any idea about that situation at Gallipolis, but most any of these other people could know something. You have to be cautious."

"How many castaways have you counted today?" Susie asked Becky as she joined her beside Matt's wagon.

To pass the time they had started tallying the items that had been thrown away by previous emigrants. Glancing at the mules, who were laboring to pull their vehicle, Becky could understand why the other wagons had to be lightened. She wondered vaguely what she and Matt had that could possibly be discarded. They had very few clothes left, and the supplies had dwindled by half now. Nothing of any weight was left, except Fluff's crate, which she couldn't bring herself to throw away, and Matt's steamboat whistle. She knew he would never leave it behind.

She shook her head. "Did you see that marble-topped dresser? The mirror is broken now, but at one time, it would have been an elegant piece of furniture. Made me almost sick to see it lying there, bleaching in the sun."

"I suppose you saw the baby's cradle. I wondered if the baby had died. Becky, this Oregon Trail does terrible things to people. I keep wondering when some of us are going to die. I overheard Luke telling Maurie that it was a miracle for us to get this distance without more deaths and sickness."

"I suppose part of the reason is that we're ahead of the other caravans, and we aren't subject to the diseases they have."

"Of course those people that Hudnall man is with are still in front of us, but there's not so many of them." Susie turned to go back to her parents' wagon, and she gasped.

"Look, Aunt Lizzie is slumped down in the seat. Has she fainted?"

Aunt Lizzie's mules were stepping along, as lively as if they had a driver, but the reins were lying loosely in the elderly woman's hands when Becky reached the wagon. "Go tell Luke, Susie. Ask Maurie to come here, if you see him."

She climbed into the wagon, took the reins from the limp hands, and felt Aunt Lizzie's chest. She could feel a heartbeat and she gasped in relief, although her friend's face wore a deathly pallor.

In a few minutes, Maurie reached her. He swung from the saddle and into the wagon in one fluid movement. "Stop the mules, Becky. I told Luke to halt until we see what's wrong. Bring some water."

Becky climbed down and dipped a tin of water from the wooden barrel on the side of the wagon. Maurie sloshed a bit of it over Aunt Lizzie's face, and she opened her eyes.

"Tryin' to drown me, young feller?" she said with a hint of her old alacrity.

He smiled. "I may have to, if you don't straighten up and drive these mules."

"My traveling days are over, Sonny. Pull my wagon to one side and go on without me. But I want to talk to Becky, first, private."

"Leave you by the trail? Forget it. I contracted to take you to Oregon, and I'm going to do it."

"No." She shook her head stubbornly. "You'll be goin' on without me, but at that, I ain't got no regrets. Had a good time these weeks, and I'm a-thankin' you for bringing me along."

Maurie picked her up and moved into the back of the wagon, placing her on a pile of quilts. "You ride back there with her, Becky, and I'll drive the mules until we camp for the night."

Maurie shouted to Luke, and the wagons moved ahead. Becky combed Aunt Lizzie's hair and kept wiping her face with a moist cloth. The woman's eyes opened occasionally and fixed Becky with a keen look.

Once she said, "It's good of him to try to help, but I know my time has come. My heart's been a-beatin' slower and slower the last few days, and every so often would just plain quit on me. That's what happened back there—I had a sinkin' spell. Becky, I've got to talk to you alone. You know what about."

Becky nodded nervously. She had enough problems without taking on Aunt Lizzie's mission to the Oregon provisional government. But she knew she had no choice, for in a weak moment she'd promised.

As soon as Maurie stopped the wagon and started to unhitch the mules Aunt Lizzie said briskly, "Quick, before someone comes. Reach under my dress and unfasten the leather packet."

Becky hesitated, thinking it unseemly for her to look upon Aunt Lizzie's body.

The old lady sensed her hesitancy. "This ain't no time for modesty. Yank that off," and she pulled her dress above her waist. Trying not to look at the bony legs and ragged bloomers, Becky unbuckled the heavy belt.

"Fasten that around your waist, and promise me you won't take it off until you place it in the hands of that Abernethy feller in Oregon City. I can't die in peace unless I know my mission's being carried out. Raise your hand and swear you'll do it, and won't tell anybody either."

Becky lifted a trembling hand. "I'll take it to Oregon City and will tell no one I have it until then."

"Becky, I'd better tell you. There's more than papers in

that belt. There's money; lots of money. Good luck to you."

Becky lifted her skirts and fastened the belt next to her skin. It felt heavy and ominous. The enormity of the task already weighed on her mind.

Glancing out of the wagon and seeing they were still alone, Becky said, "Now that I'm doing you a favor, Aunt Lizzie, I want you to do something for me. You told me once that you knew why Matt is so protective with me. He won't tell me, and I think I have the right to know."

Speaking lowly, and even that seemed an effort, Aunt Lizzie said, "Where I'm going Matt Miller can't get even with me for tellin', so I will. Becky, your mother wasn't married a second time. She thought the Norwegian sailor was goin' to marry her, and she got in the family way. But when he found out you were on the way, he just eased out and left her."

"But what does that have to do with me?" she whispered hoarsely. "I can't help what my mother did."

"No, but she was afraid you'd follow in her footsteps, and she made Matt promise that he'd keep you from harm. Matt hasn't had an easy life, Becky. He 'most worshiped his mother, and he nearly went out of his mind when he learned what she'd done."

"Poor Matt. And I haven't made his life any easier."

"He loved you right from the first, child. And he'd rather you didn't know. They left Philadelphia to keep you from finding out. Your mother told me about it herself. Don't tell him I told you."

The last words were barely more than a whisper, and Becky turned gladly when Reverend and Mrs. Hopkins appeared at the wagon flap.

"Would you like me to pray, Aunt Lizzie?" the preacher asked.

She nodded, whispering. "I'm ready to go, Preacher. Made peace with my Maker a long time ago. I've tried to lend a hand where it was needed."

"You've been a big help to me, Aunt Lizzie, and I've waited too long to tell you so. Been just like my own grandmother."

"You're a good child, Becky. And you're going to have a good life in Oregon. You'll be all right."

Those were the last words the dying woman spoke, although she breathed on for a few more hours.

My final break with the past, Becky thought as she listened to the short service Reverend Hopkins was saying over Aunt Lizzie's still body. Although she mourned the loss of her friend, Becky shed no tears.

"Do you know any of her kin that should be notified?" Maurie asked when they stopped for the nooning.

"She had a sister in Pittsburgh and a son living near Nashville," Matt answered. "I suppose we can try to send a message at the next fort."

"What about her effects?" Maurie wondered. "Is there anything we should send back?"

Maurie had driven the wagon that morning, and he had detailed Rusty to drive during the afternoon. "Maybe some of you women can look the wagon over," he said to Becky, "and we'll see what she had with her."

"Will it be all right to wait until we arrive at South Pass? We'll stop there for a few day's rest, won't we?"

"Sure, that will be fine."

Another fire! Becky heard the words sounding around the camp circle, and she chilled at the thought as she drew on a dress. She knew she'd been asleep for hours.

Susie was running toward her when she stepped outside the wagon. "It's Aunt Lizzie's wagon, Becky. Father saw it. Too late to save anything in it, looks like."

Men were running with buckets of water to stop the blaze, but when the fire was doused, nothing was left except a charred frame.

Maurie followed Matt to his wagon. "Matt, that fire had to have been started deliberately. Could there have been something in that wagon that someone wanted to destroy?"

"I haven't any idea," Matt assured him.

Becky slipped quietly into their wagon, but she noted Maurie's probing glance in her direction. The belt around her waist felt heavy as lead. Whoever had burned that wagon must have expected to destroy any message Aunt Lizzie carried, and if someone was that desperate, what would happen if *she* came under suspicion? She longed to share her dilemma with Matt and Maurie and let them wrestle with the problem, but she refused to place either man in danger.

Aunt Lizzie's death left a void in Becky's life; still she rejoiced that her friend's last days had been happy. Even if she hadn't lived to complete her task, she'd enjoyed those hazardous days crossing the plains, fording dangerous rivers, going on a buffalo hunt, and glorying in her first sight of the Rockies.

It wasn't Aunt Lizzie's death that caused Becky's wakeful nights. The revelation about her own illegitimacy had stunned Becky, bringing a resentment against her mother for passing such a heritage to her. She had loved her mother, whose care through the early years of Becky's life had been warm and tender. No girl could have asked for a more affectionate parent. Now Becky found it difficult to have one pleasant thought of her.

As for her father! *Coward, scoundrel, villain, rascal, black-*

guard, scum of the earth: She couldn't think of enough vile names to call him. How dare he walk off and leave a woman in the family way?

The fact that she looked like him infuriated Becky. Did she resemble him in other ways, too? Was she like her mother? Was Matt justified in accusing her of being wanton? What if she'd inherited the undesirable characteristics of *both* parents?

She flushed with embarrassment when she remembered how she felt when Maurie held and kissed her. Was she any better than her mother? What if the circumstances had been different, and Maurie hadn't been reluctant the times they'd been alone?

Becky couldn't face the answers to those questions, and worry over her past added one more tedium to the exhausting journey. Shame strained her relations with Maurie. He gave her more than one questioning glance when they met, but Becky turned away with a burning face.

The ascent to South Pass was so gradual that Becky often had to remind herself that they were climbing the mountains, although she only had to take a look at the gaunt, struggling mules to know they were gaining altitude. South Pass was a windswept meadow that offered plenty of good grazing for the animals. The mules wouldn't eat the abundant sagebrush, but Becky liked the purple bloom that permeated the campsite with a spicy fragrance. Besides the sagebrush, wildflowers grew in profusion—blue lupines, red Indian paintbrush, and dozens of varieties that no one could name.

Susie and Becky explored the pass on foot after Luke assured them they wouldn't encounter any snakes at that altitude. Stretched out on their backs among the flowers, they watched white clouds moving fleetingly across the azure sky. Becky added dozens of pictures to her portfolio, but she didn't paint the ranges of mountains far to the west. Realizing that they had to cross those mountains filled her with dread, and she wouldn't ruin her few days of rest by trying to place them on canvas.

One afternoon, perched on a high rock that overlooked the campsite, Becky sketched the wagon train, finding it difficult to comprehend that this was the same group of people who had left Independence three months ago. Some of the wagons were wrecks. The ragged canvases had been patched as long as the women could find mending materials, but when no fabric remained, the holes gapped, allowing the sun and rain to infiltrate their belongings.

Supplies, too, had dwindled at a rapid rate, and it was well enough that the wagons had less to carry, for the broken wheels were tied together with wire. Mules' hooves were cracked and sore, and during the rest stop, the men wrapped buffalo hides around the mules' feet.

The emigrants didn't look any better than their wagons. Did anyone have a garment that wasn't tattered and patched? Even the desire for clean clothes had ebbed, for the women were often too weary to wash when there was water, and maybe the tattered garment wouldn't hold together for one more washing anyway.

Becky and Susie had worn out all their shoes and would have been forced to walk barefooted if Maurie hadn't produced some boots from one of his wagons. They were uncomfortable, but Becky was thankful to have anything to cover her feet.

Looking at her canvas after three hours of sketching, Becky considered destroying it, for she doubted that this was the sort of record Mr. Hamilton wanted of the Oregon Trail. He would no doubt consider its horrors unrealistic, but she added it to her large carton of sketches.

Becky heard the barking dogs and thought she was dreaming of Fluff again, until she realized that she had been awakened by sounds outside the wagon. Peering out, she saw that the area had been overrun by Indians, and she smothered a shriek until she saw Maurie and Luke moving easily among the newcomers. Apparently these were old friends, so Becky dressed hurriedly, welcoming the opportunity to see Indians at close range.

Matt was advancing toward the group when Becky joined him.

"These are friendly Indians," Maurie explained, noting the skeptical expression on Matt's face. "They're of the Shoshone tribe; Luke and I have wintered with them many seasons." He drew Matt out of hearing of the others. "And they've confirmed our suspicions. That group Hudnall was with had their wagons full of guns, and they've given them to Indians, telling them to prevent the passage of any more wagons."

"I see some of these men have new guns."

"Yes, but they traded those for horses. Best I can figure, they've distributed all the guns, except one wagon that headed north from here, toward the Crow tribes. They abandoned their wagons, traded guns for horses, and started out on horseback."

"Heading for Oregon, I suppose, to be paid for their services."

Maurie nodded savagely. "And leaving a legacy of potential death and destruction for American emigrants. I wish I'd been more alert to what was going on. Perhaps we could have stopped them. When I think of how many

Americans may die because of British selfishness, I have a feeling I'm not going to remain neutral much longer in this conflict."

Becky brightened a bit. Perhaps even yet she could enlist Maurie's help in getting Polk's message and money to Oregon.

Becky hadn't had the nerve to look closely at what she carried. One day she had peered in cautiously, and the sight of a hundred-dollar bill had frightened her so that she had hastily refastened the belt. She'd be happier if she didn't know how much money she was carrying around her waist.

"These Indians have items to trade, Matt, if you're interested. You might pass the word."

"We don't have much left, except foodstuffs, and I hesitate to trade any of them off, but we'll see what they have."

Susie came running, wearing a pair of moccasins that her father had bartered for.

"Look, Becky. Maybe Matt will buy something for you before they trade all their things."

The newcomers numbered about thirty, and Maurie explained that they were members of the same family. The men were dressed in buckskin breeches much like the ones Maurie and Luke wore, but they were naked above the waist, except for bear-claw necklaces. The women wore breeches also, but they had on tuniclike shirts that hung almost to their knees. A few children were naked and none too clean, Becky decided, her nose dilating at the mixture of grease and smoke that pervaded the area. Two tepees had been set up, leading Becky to wonder how long the Indians might be intending to stay.

In her haste to see the Indians, Becky hadn't braided her hair or twisted it into a bun, and the long, blond hair must have been a source of wonder to the Indians, for the women crowded around her, lifting the gleaming tresses, rubbing her hair in the palms of their hands.

Matt frowned, and Becky knew he didn't like their familiar actions, and truthfully, she didn't appreciate the attention either. But she caught Maurie's eye, and when he shook his head cautiously, Becky tried not to cringe as one of the women ran a hand over her face. The other emigrant women received their share of attention, and Becky realized that the Indians were only curious.

After eating a hasty breakfast, Becky took her painting materials and moved around the campsite, sketching the Indians. One boy, in his early teens, stood diffidently surveying the scene. As Becky sketched his proud bearing, his broad shoulders, the haughty look in his eyes, she was suddenly aware of how much the boy looked like Luke.

Becky's thoughts did a double take. *Luke!* Where was he? Looking around the camp she saw Luke and one of the Indian women riding away. Was she Luke's Indian wife? Was this boy his son?

She felt suddenly sick to her stomach, and perspiration wet her palms. Her eyes blurred. What was bothering her? As hard as she tried to stifle it, the thought invaded her mind, *Does Maurie have an Indian wife, too? Is that why he won't make a commitment to me?* Revolted at the thought, Becky wandered away from the main group of Indians, who were bargaining with the emigrants.

Hardly conscious of where she was going, Becky heard barking again, and she turned toward the sound. Nestled in the grass, a dog was playing with her pups—four round balls of gray fur tumbling and rolling on the ground. Dropping to her knees, Becky reached for one—a half-grown pup, already bigger than Fluff had ever been. His long nose, gangly legs, big feet, and friendly brown eyes won her immediately. The dog was mostly gray, with white spots on his back.

Becky spent hours playing with the dogs, trying to forget her suspicions about Maurie. She didn't mingle with the Indians again, but Susie came by to report, "A few of our people have traded for horses—traded off things they'd have to throw away anyway. Sam Johnson got a black horse in exchange for a large mirror. Mrs. Johnson looked sorry to lose the mirror, but the horse probably will do them more good."

On her next trip, Susie said, "That one woman over there, who makes Maurie's buckskins, has a white doeskin outfit that I'd love to have, but I know I'm too fat for it. Several of the women have tried to trade her out of it, but she keeps shaking her head. It would fit you, I think. Why don't you tell Matt to trade for it?"

Becky knew which woman Susie meant, for earlier in the day she had sketched her stirring a pot of food over the open fire. Could *this* woman be Maurie's companion? No, she looked much older than Maurie.

But Becky wasn't interested in the doeskin garment. She wanted one of the dogs, and she wondered if Matt would let her have one.

Susie was sitting beside her when the Indians prepared to leave. "Say," she whispered, "that woman with the doeskin outfit is coming this way. Look how pretty it is."

Becky, holding one of the pups in her lap, glanced up as the woman stopped in front of her. Thrusting the soft doeskin dress toward Becky, the woman said, "Gift. Gift."

"Why, I can't take it as a gift. Matt will pay you."

Shaking her head, the brown face expressed her will. "No. No. Gift. Pretty hair, pretty face. Take."

Becky glanced over the woman's shoulder and intercepted Maurie's gaze. His eyes flashed a message, and she reddened. Of course, he'd arranged for her to have the garment without Matt's suspecting. But she wasn't sure Maurie hadn't underestimated her brother's suspicious nature.

She took the garment from the woman, noting that Matt had observed the scene without objecting.

"Thank you," she said, wishing she could give the woman a gift. Then she thought of the portrait she had painted in the morning. She motioned Maurie to come to her, and she asked him, "Would she like this sketch I made of her?"

His beaming smile left no doubt of the answer. "Ask her."

Becky held out the picture to the woman, whose face was expressionless at first as she looked in bewilderment at her likeness. Then she ran to the mirror an Indian was loading on his horse. She stooped to look at herself in it, then looked at the painting Becky had done. Showing the picture to the other Indians, her voice raised in high-pitched tones that bore the unmistakable sounds of delight.

The Indians were departing at last, and Becky reluctantly released the pup she held so that the owner could place him into a basket on the back of a travois. The dog barked at her, and Becky's eyes misted, but instead of turning away, she watched the Indians leave, feeling disconsolate and lonely.

A male Indian swung on the bareback horse that was attached to the travois, waved farewell to Luke and Maurie, and kicked the horse into action. But Maurie halted him and spoke, gesturing toward the basket of dogs.

"No, Maurie, don't be a fool!" Luke growled.

But Maurie ignored him, holding up a knife he slipped

from his belt. Some kind of deal was being made, which obviously displeased Luke, for he swore disgustedly.

Maurie knelt beside the travois, and lifting the lid of the basket, he turned to Becky. "Which one do you want?"

Only a moment was needed for Becky to overcome her surprise, and she reached quickly and grabbed the gray dog.

"You know they're part wolf, Maurie; you're asking for trouble with the livestock."

"The other dog didn't cause any trouble."

"No, but she had him trained before we started out."

Matt became aware of what was going on and thrust himself into the argument. "What's this, Davis? I don't want her to have a dog."

"Well, if you could stand there and see the expression on her face and the woebegone look in those blue eyes while she watched the dogs being taken away, it was more than I could do."

Matt glanced toward Becky, who fiercely clutched the dog in her arms, and apparently decided further argument was useless, so he turned away. But Becky didn't like his shrewd, angry glance at Maurie. Fearing Matt still might try to make her give up the dog, Becky scampered toward the wagon and placed the dog in Fluff's crate.

Becky didn't try to thank Maurie until after dark, when she knew Matt would be on night duty. Maurie saw her coming toward him, and he motioned her away from the wagons. The darkness surrounded them, but with her hand in his, Becky wasn't afraid.

He stopped at last, and they sat on a rock outcropping.

"Thank you, Maurie. Those two words sound pretty inadequate for what I feel. The doeskin garment is beautiful, with all that beaded work, and it fits me perfectly.

Don't know when I'll have the nerve to wear it, but I will. And you alone knew how much I wanted the dog."

His arms went around her shoulders, and he drew her toward him. Chuckling, he said, "Have you named him?"

"Sure. Don't you think *Shoshone* would be a good name?"

"None better," he said. "I think everyone else in the caravan is mad at me, but if you're happy, I don't care."

"I'm happy."

Maurie turned her face to his and lowered his lips. She stiffened at first, wondering about an Indian wife, but she couldn't ask. After all, she had no right to pry into his past. As she surrendered to the ardor of his caresses, frighteningly vivid emotions stirred in Becky. She had learned so much on this journey, but it seemed that she still had much to learn about her body. The sensations Maurie's hands and lips aroused didn't lessen, even after they returned to the wagons, and Becky was awake most of the night, wondering what had happened to her.

Had her mother experienced similar feelings that led to her relationship with the Norwegian sailor? Becky sobbed out her frustration, hoping Matt wouldn't hear. She struggled with the words of Jesus, "But if ye forgive not . . . , neither will your Father forgive your trespasses."

When the storm of anguish passed, Becky realized the tears had washed away much of her resentment against her mother. Even the hatred for her father had disappeared. After all, who was she to judge her parents? For once Matt had been right, she admitted—she would have been better off not to know the details of her birth.

Toward morning, a new thought intruded: When Maurie's hands had moved over her back, had he felt the thick money belt she carried?

10

Nothing Becky had experienced prepared her for the desolate Sublette Cutoff. Maurie had elected to take the fifty-mile grassless trail because it shortened the trip by a week, but before the first day was over Becky doubted his judgment.

Maurie had gambled that there would be enough grazing and water, but for two nights, dry camps were necessary, and during these stops there was little cooking and no washing. The water they carried in barrels had to be reserved for the livestock and occasional sips of water for themselves. Several emigrants gave Becky dirty looks when they saw her watering Shoshone, but since she shared her own scant portion with the dog, she didn't consider she was depriving anyone else. It was a poor time to adopt a puppy, she knew, but the dog seemed to bear the torturous trail better than any of the other animals.

Becky slept very little during the crossing, for in addition to her own discomfort, the mules brayed and the cattle bawled all night long. Many weaker mules and cattle died along this stretch of the trail, and Matt worried that his mules wouldn't last out the journey. The caravan's progress had slowed considerably, for not only was the trail rougher and steeper, but the mules had little strength left.

On the third morning, when they started to pull out, Becky noticed the *Allegheny*'s whistle lying beside the trail.

"Matt," she cried. "You aren't leaving the whistle?"

His eyes were wretched, and he threaded fingers through his hair. "What else can I do, Becky? There's nothing left in the wagon but our food. We can't throw it away, and we have to lighten the load some way. The mules have had all they can take."

Becky tugged on the whistle until she lifted it, and she carried it to the wagon. "Matt, I won't let you throw this away. You've given up everything else because of me. You have to have something left. Haul this in the wagon today, and tonight I'll have Luke or Maurie make a little travois for me, like the Indians use. I'll drag the whistle to Oregon."

The very fact that Matt acquiesced was evidence of how much he wanted to take the whistle. In spite of his concern for the mules, he appeared lighthearted the rest of the day.

Numerous canyons, all of which looked alike to Becky, surrounded them, and she was amazed that Luke and Maurie always chose the right one. In places the passages were barely wide enough for a wagon, and sometimes the gullies on each side of the trail were so deep that Becky held her breath, fearing Matt's wagon would hurtle over the brink.

The trail fever Luke had predicted started to afflict the

emigrants. Tempers flared between families and friends. Conversation remained at a minimum, but most words uttered were angry and complaining. Through it all, Maurie remained calm and unperturbed.

In addition to the rough terrain, Shoshone had proved to be a nuisance from the first. He often barked day and night, keeping Matt's mules restless. He chewed up Becky's moccasins, and when he was loose, he chased everyone who came by.

Matt's patience broke, and he threatened to dispose of the dog if Becky didn't control him, but he was such a lively animal that she didn't know what she could do.

Maurie must have become aware of the dissension, for he approached their campfire when Becky was holding the pup to keep him from annoying the Hopkins, who had stopped for a visit. Shoshone broke loose from Becky to tug on Maurie's pants.

"Becky, why don't you keep the dog on a leash, the way you did Fluff?"

She decided he was getting tired of Shoshone, too, and answered sulkily, "I don't have a collar for him. I still have the leash, but Fluff had on his collar when. . .," her voice trailed off; she couldn't talk about Fluff even yet.

"I think I can do something about that," Maurie assured her. He was gone for a short while, and when he returned, he had a length of braided leather in his hand. Kneeling beside her, he measured the leather around Shoshone's neck, saying, "I thought this would be about the right size. Hold the ends while I trim it and insert a metal ring for the leash."

When he finished, he placed the collar around Shoshone's neck, as the dog slept peacefully in Becky's lap. She had to exert all her willpower to keep from running her hands through Maurie's dark hair. Her breathing was rapid, and she thought Maurie must have realized her plight, for before she was tempted further, he rose quickly.

"That should keep him under control."

At that moment Becky was mostly concerned about her own control, but she quietly murmured her thanks as Matt added, "Thanks, Maurie. I should have thought to make a collar myself."

Becky kept her eyes on the dog, for her heart was beating at such a rapid rate she thought she might suffocate.

Once the cutoff was behind them, the emigrants began to look forward to arriving at Fort Hall, which they reached on August 5, and none too soon either, for the morning after they halted their wagons in front of the primitive structure, Rose Cox's labor pains started.

Becky had watched the young woman for days, wondering how she could endure the discomfort of the trail. Her body was so cumbersome that she scarcely moved without Jed's help, and although, like the rest of the women, she tried to walk to spare the mules, the last ten days she had lain in the wagon. When they'd left Independence, Rose's hair had been shining, and her skin pure and soft, but now it was stringy and lifeless; her skin was mottled with red splotches, and her body was misshapen and gruesome.

So it was a relief for Becky to see Jed hurrying across the camp to Mrs. Hopkins, for from Rose's calculations, the baby was long overdue. Perhaps to avoid exposing Susie to the birthing, Mrs. Hopkins suggested to her husband that he should take Becky and Susie into the fort.

The first person Becky saw was Kenneth Hudnall, who approached them with a bland smile. Becky hadn't noticed Hudnall's crinkled, tiny ears before, but they did little to enhance his profile.

"Glad to see you, Reverend, and you, ladies," he said, doffing his hat. "Had a rough journey?"

"Yes, we have, but the Lord has brought us through without mishap."

Suavely, Hudnall said, "I wish I could tell you the worst is over, but the road from here on to Oregon—if one could call it a road—is impossible to cross. My friends and I started out on horseback, didn't even try to take our wagons, and we were forced to turn back. There was one dangerous river after another, and the Indians are more hostile than those back on the plains."

Especially after you provided them with guns, Becky wanted to say, but she knew she shouldn't divulge what Maurie had learned about Hudnall and his friends.

Reverend Hopkins listened politely to Hudnall's tale of woe, before he said, "If we've made it this far, we'll go on. Only about three hundred more miles to go, I think, and we should make that in a month."

"Of course, many emigrants turn south here and go into the Spanish territory of California. The trail is much easier and water more plentiful. And the Spanish welcome settlers."

So that's Hudnall's game! Since the Indians hadn't been able to halt Maurie's caravan, the British were now trying to divert the emigrants to California. As disgruntled as some of their fellow travelers had become, Becky wouldn't be surprised if Hudnall convinced some of them.

The fort, an outpost of the Hudson's Bay Company, was better equipped than Fort Laramie, but since the British were hardly civil to the emigrants, they didn't tarry long inside the walls of the fort. Becky had hoped that Rose's baby would have arrived by the time they returned, but Mrs. Hopkins met them, a worried expression on her face.

"Alvin, do you think there might be a doctor at the fort? Rose is having trouble, and neither Mrs. Johnson nor I know what to do. See if Maurie can help us."

Maurie came immediately, saying, "Last year there was an old doctor at the fort. I'll go see. How long is this going to take?"

Mrs. Hopkins spread her hands wide. "I've no idea. She's in mortal agony; I don't think she can stand much more pain."

Rose uttered a piercing scream that echoed around the campsite, and cold prickles coursed down Becky's back. Maurie swung into his saddle and raced toward the fort. He was back in a short time with a rum-soaked old man, so bleary-eyed and untidy that Becky had little hope of any help from him.

Perhaps the young woman had been beyond help, but a few hours after giving birth to a stillborn daughter, Rose died also. Mrs. Hopkins looked devastated when she brought Becky and Susie the news.

"Poor Jed," she said. "He's blaming himself, of course, and I don't know how he'll stand this sorrow. He raved and ranted when the doctor told him she was dying, but once she passed away, he quieted down. Even after we prepared the body for burial, he sat and stared. He won't speak; he won't even take a drink of water. Alvin and Maurie are going to sit with him tonight."

Rose and her daughter were buried in the little cemetery outside the walls of the fort, with only a few of the emigrants present, for Maurie hadn't thought it wise to leave the wagons unattended so close to the British fort. Becky didn't hear a word of Reverend Hopkins's service; she couldn't take her eyes from Jed's haggard face. He stared at the open grave, his hands shaking, tears rolling over his cheeks.

Never before had Becky heard the camp as quiet as it was that night. The travelers spoke in whispers as they prepared for tomorrow's journey. Long after she should have been asleep, Becky mourned for Rose, and her heart was full of sympathy for Jed, who must go on alone.

"Hudnall was right, wasn't he?" Susie said as she plodded along beside Becky. Fort Hall was a week behind them, and the trail was barely passable. More than once, Maurie and Luke had blasted rocks from the roadbed to allow the wagons to pass, and Becky learned that she couldn't drag the travois over the rough ground. Many times, when they were behind the wagon and Matt couldn't see, she and Susie lifted the heavy steamboat whistle and carried it. She was determined that the *Allegheny*'s whistle would someday announce the arrival of a steamboat on the Columbia. She was going to take the whistle with her, though her strength was lessening more each day. For by the time she carried the whistle and tried to keep Shoshone out of mischief, at the end of the day, Becky was exhausted.

The dog had aggravated Matt from the first, and Becky felt sure he was jealous because Maurie had given her the pup. Well, at least, Shoshone took care of his own baths, so she didn't have to depend on Matt providing water to keep this dog clean.

When she'd had the animal a month, Becky knew Luke had been right. While the emigrants and mules languished, Shoshone grew like a weed, and his wild nature surfaced often. The dog was unhappy sleeping in the wagon, so Becky started tying him outside at night. That worked all right until the night a pack of coyotes circled the camp, and Shoshone answered their chorus by barking all night. From the indignant glances the emigrants cast his way the next morning, while Shoshone slept peacefully under the wagon, Becky was sure no one in camp had slept much.

Now he was howling again! Becky scurried out of her bed, and with an effort, lifted the heavy dog into the wagon. That muffled his barking, but she couldn't sleep, nor could Matt, apparently.

Pounding on the side of the wagon, her brother delivered an ultimatum. "Keep that dog quiet, or I'm going to shoot him."

Coming in from night guard, Maurie heard the commotion, and he strolled over. "I've an idea that might quiet him, Matt."

"You'd better have, Davis," Matt said in surly tones. He always called Maurie by his last name when he was out of sorts. "This is all your fault, for Luke and I both tried to keep you from giving her this mongrel."

"I know," Maurie said, laughing good-naturedly. "I take all the blame. Open the curtains, Becky. I think I can quiet him."

She slipped under the quilts as he reached in for Shoshone. "What are you going to do to him?" she questioned sharply.

"Put a muzzle on him. Here, Matt, hold the dog while I tie this leather around his mouth." Shoshone struggled violently, but at last they had the dog's mouth tied securely with leather thongs, which they fastened to his collar.

Shoshone was mute, but he wasn't happy, and the rest of the night, he pawed at the contraption over his mouth, whining so piteously that Becky cried. She knew better than to risk Matt's ire by turning him loose, but by morning, she was tense and resentful. As soon as she heard Matt stirring beneath the wagon, she dressed and took Shoshone outside. Since it was daylight, she hoped everyone would be awake, but she didn't intend to have the dog persecuted any longer.

As soon as Becky unfastened the muzzle, whether in suppressed resentment over Matt's part in muzzling him or because Matt happened to be the only one near, Shoshone suddenly reached out and nipped him on the leg.

In disbelief, Matt said, "Why, that mutt bit me!" He angrily jerked his pants leg out of Shoshone's mouth, and when Becky sensed his intent, she reached down and seized the dog just as Matt kicked. Instead of hitting the dog, his foot landed on her forearm. Her shrill scream of pain resounded through the camp, and Maurie rolled out of his blankets and came running.

"What's going on here?" he demanded.

"He's trying to kill my dog," she shouted, quickly putting Shoshone in the wagon. She could feel a bump rising on her arm, and she rubbed it gingerly.

Matt looked guilty, but he was on the defensive. "That dog bit me, and I won't have him around here any longer. It was your idea to bring him along—you get rid of him."

Maurie ignored Matt when he noticed Becky rubbing her arm. "What's the matter with your arm?"

She dropped her hand instantly. "Nothing!" Under no circumstances would she foster a fight between her brother and the man she loved.

The emigrants were gathering around them, and Maurie pleaded, his eyes tender and loving. "We will have to do something with him, Becky, for I can't have the whole camp in an uproar."

Tears glistened in her eyes, and she shook her head. "No. No."

"All the dog needs is a good working," a new voice commented. Everyone turned to look at Rusty Smith. He so seldom said anything that Maurie and Matt seemed inclined to listen.

"He'd make a good cow dog if someone would train him, and I'll do it. Let me take him out with the herd every morning, and he'll be so tired at night, he won't feel like barking."

Becky's tired eyes brightened a little. "You won't hurt him?" She sniffed.

Rusty spat a generous portion of tobacco juice on the ground before he assured her, "Naw. Be good for him."

"Just as soon as I feed him, you can take him."

As soon as they were alone, Matt lifted her sleeve to see the red, rapidly swelling knot on her arm. A wretched look of pain and remorse crossed his face, but he made no apology, simply pulled down her sleeve and moved away. Becky didn't hold the incident against Matt—just another result of trail fever.

True to Rusty's prediction, Shoshone came in from the herd exhausted, and not a sound was heard from him all night. With the dog's problem solved, Becky hoped she wouldn't have any more worries, except how to cross a couple hundred barren miles.

"Tomorrow, we'll arrive at Fort Boise and our last chance to do any resting before we reach the Blue Mountains," Maurie told them at their final camp along the Snake River.

For miles they'd traveled along the high bluffs surrounding the river, and they'd had to climb down on foot to the water. Although they drank their fill, by the time they reached the wagons, they felt thirsty again.

"I'm going hunting while we're camped at the fort," Luke announced. "Maurie and I are out of meat, and we might find some mountain goats or sheep in this area. Possibly some elk, too. Anybody want to go with me?"

"Yeah, I'll go," Matt said. "We have some salt pork left, but I'd like some fresh meat."

Two other emigrants wanted to go hunting also, and the four of them left before daybreak their second day at the fort.

About noon, Maurie strolled by where Becky was trying to mend a dress she had washed.

"Want to go exploring with me?"

Becky hesitated, and Maurie gave her an intense look. She feared to be alone with him now that she suspected she might have inherited her mother's promiscuity.

At first she thought she would say she was tired, but the day's rest had restored her energy, and there was no need to add lying to her doubtful characteristics. Why not accept her heritage for what it was and rely on her own good sense to deal with situations when they arose? She couldn't do one thing about her past, but she could be master of her future. She had slowly come to the conclusion that her feelings toward Maurie were normal reactions, as long as she approached them in the right way.

These thoughts flitted through her mind so rapidly that in less than a minute she jumped up eagerly, and said, "Let's go."

"Bring your paints then; you may want to record what we see."

"What is it?" she demanded as she lifted her satchel

from the wagon. Taking it, Maurie smiled. "Wait, and see."

Maurie followed the small creek they were camped beside, and as soon as they were out of sight of the wagons, he took her hand.

"Matt made this easy for me by deciding to go hunting. He guards you like a watchdog, but maybe it's a good thing."

The creek was a noisy, rocky stream, but after a while, Becky noted that the water was placid, and rounding a curve, they came to a small lake. At first she couldn't understand what was so great about this lake, but suddenly comprehending, she glanced quickly at Maurie, her eyes alight with interest.

A beaver dam! She followed Maurie downstream until they were opposite the dam, and she sank down in the thick grass, reaching for her paint and brushes. The flow of the creek had been stopped by a barrier of logs and mud placed at a narrow ford, and dotted around the water were mounds of the same type of earthen construction. Soon several young beaver came out to play on one of the mounds.

"I'll not disturb you, Becky. Paint as long as you like," Maurie said, and he leaned back against a tree and closed his eyes.

After Becky had painted several sketches of the beavers, she turned her attention to Maurie. Taking out a rather large piece of paper, she unrolled it, laid it on the grass, and studied him intently.

His skin was only a shade lighter than his hair after months of exposure to nature's onslaughts; his hair hung loosely over his shoulders, several inches longer than when they'd left Independence. He was clean and neat after a bath in the creek and a change into some new buckskins he'd gotten from the Indian woman at South Pass. Becky transferred his likeness to the canvas.

Perhaps aware of her close scrutiny, Maurie opened his eyes, and his expression conveyed a message she couldn't interpret.

"Don't move," she said. "Keep your eyes open, but don't move. I'm almost finished."

When she laid down her brush, Maurie joined her. "Oh, painting my picture, huh?" Pulling on one of her braids, he said, "I brought you here to paint the beaver dam."

"Which I did," Becky said, exhibiting the sketches she'd done. "This is such a beautiful place. Have you been here before?"

"Many times. This is one of the first streams I trapped when I came to the mountains. Makes me kind of sick, Becky, when I remember how many beaver there used to be. A man could take dozens of pelts in a few days, but the beaver are nearly gone now."

"You miss it, don't you?"

"Miss it?" He laughed in wonder. "Nothing else could compare with that type of life for a young man.

"Along about September, we'd make up into small companies of four or five men and head for the mountains, trapping as we went. Always moving on. When the streams froze, and we couldn't trap, we'd go into winter quarters in a sheltered place like this and wait until spring. Along about the middle of summer, we'd go to rendezvous."

"I don't know what a rendezvous is."

"Nobody could, without attending one. Thousands of people around—trappers, hunters, traders, and Indians from dozens of tribes. Horse racing, drinking, gambling, contests of all kinds made it a carnival atmosphere. Many a man lost his whole year's work in a few days of carousing, but Luke guided me well, and I escaped all that. The last rendezvous was five years ago, and it was dull compared to the first one I attended."

"Do you still wish you were trapping?" Becky asked, pulling up blades of grass and shaping them into tiny ringlets.

Maurie lay back, hands under his head. "No, I guess not, for I'm looking forward to living in Oregon. A trapper's life was good for me, though, and I loved it because it helped me to forget the past."

Although she had vowed not to ask, she did. "Maurie, did you ever have an Indian wife? I couldn't help notice the boy at South Pass who looked so much like Luke. I guess that was part of a trapper's life, too."

"Well, it wasn't part of mine." He rolled on his side and looked at her with longing. "Becky, do you know you've never told me you love me? You've acted the part, but you never say the words."

"That kind of talk doesn't come easily for me, but I think about it a lot. In a way, to say, 'I love you,' is a weak phrase to explain how you've invaded my mind, my heart, my body. Sometimes I remind myself of a little duck we had on the steamboat one year." She laughed shyly. "I suppose you'd think the comparison is silly."

Taking her hand, he said, "Tell me."

"The first year we were on the *Allegheny*, a wild duck came to live with us. Matt thought she'd probably fallen behind during the southern migration. She stayed for a couple of seasons, and although she would quack when other ducks flew over, she seemed content to stay on the boat.

"One spring a wild drake landed on the pilothouse, and our duck took an interest in him at once. They'd fly together ahead of the boat, but at night she'd return to us.

This went on for a week or more; then one day, the drake approached and hovered over the boat, but he didn't land. Our duck quacked a few times, flew to him, and they started north together.

"Somehow I knew she wouldn't come back that time, for she'd found her mate and was willing to leave the security of the boat to head into the unknown." Her voice deepened as she spoke, and she turned to the man at her side. "Maurie, that's how I feel about you. You're the only man I've known that made me want to fly away with him."

Maurie's eyes darkened with passion, and he pulled her into his arms. "Oh, Becky, sweetheart, what a beautiful way to tell me of your love! I only hope that drake didn't have a broken wing."

Becky didn't try to figure out what he meant, for his caresses plunged her into a world of fantasy, where no problems or barriers existed. She had wondered what God's purpose was for her life, and now she knew. In Maurie's arms, she'd found her reason for being. For this she'd taken the Oregon Trail!

Maurie lifted his head, and Becky felt a rough hand on her shoulder. The rough hand belonged to Matt, and he pulled Becky to her feet, but Becky broke away from his grasp. His angry words came in gasps, and she realized her brother was almost in tears.

"Becky, how could you? After all I've done for your protection, how could you play the harlot when I left you alone for a few hours? Must I watch you all the time?"

"But Matt, we haven't done anything wrong. He was only kissing me, and if you must know, it isn't the first time. We love each other, so why shouldn't he kiss me? I don't have a husband."

Matt grazed Maurie with a contemptuous glance. "No, you don't have a husband, but he *does* have a wife."

Becky's spirits drooped, and she felt faint. Matt had spoken with such conviction. Becky's eyes focused on Maurie's face. One look at him was all Becky needed to be convinced of the truth of Matt's words. Maurie's face was chalk white, his eyes dark pools of misery.

"Maurie, how could you deceive me like this?" she whispered.

His voice was lifeless. "It's not what you think, Becky, and if he hadn't interrupted, I would have told you myself." He swung toward Matt. "And how does it happen that you know so much about my business?"

"I've known since the first day I saw you in Independence. When I entered that shack where you were signing up emigrants, I heard you tell Luke, 'I have a wife, whether I can live with her or not. I'm sick of women, and I never expect to touch another one.' If I hadn't heard that, do you think I'd have trusted you around Becky as much as I have?" He shook his fist at Maurie. "How I'd like to batter that face of yours, but we have to depend on you to take us to Oregon."

Both men turned in amazement when Becky screamed shrilly and ran toward the picture she'd painted of Maurie. She stamped her feet on his face, and taking up the paper, she mutilated it completely. Tears ran from her eyes, but she seemed unaware of them, as she turned on Matt and Maurie.

"I suppose you're satisfied, Matt Miller, that you've finally ruined my life." Swinging toward Maurie, she closed her eyes, unwilling to even see his face, "And as for you, I'll never forgive you. Don't either one of you ever speak to me again."

Grabbing her satchel of paints and the sketches of the beavers, she ran toward camp, angrily ignoring Maurie's agonized plea, "Becky, wait a minute. You don't understand."

Matt caught up with her before she reached the wagons. He grabbed her by the shoulders and turned her to face him. "And I suppose *you're* satisfied that you've finally brought us to shame, carrying on with a married man. Blood will tell every time."

Angrily, Becky broke away from his grasp. "Go on and say it. Say I'm like my mother! But it isn't the truth, if that's what you're suggesting. I'm not going to give you another baby to enslave."

Matt's face paled when she mentioned their mother. "How'd you know about that?"

Becky pushed her tumbled hair away from her face. She felt suffocated, and she jerked at her collar. "Doesn't matter. I know, and I'm tired of your insinuations about her and me. You hate her, don't you? Admit it."

"No, I don't hate her," Matt said with difficulty. "But she did disappoint me. In my sight she was perfect until she took up with that scoundrel."

"But that scoundrel happens to be my father."

"I know. Don't you think I'm reminded of that every time I look at you? He was a handsome devil—no wonder she fell for him."

The fracas had exhausted Becky, and she said wearily, "But can't you see, Matt? You were jealous of him. Can't you understand that they might have loved each other?"

"There's a right and wrong way to love," Matt declared, his visage unrelenting.

"I doubt you're capable of judging that! Have you ever seen a woman you desired? Someone you felt drawn toward?"

"Never. She cured me of that."

"Then you're the one who's out of step. It isn't the rest

of us, and I want you to leave me alone. I might make some mistakes, but they'll be *my* mistakes."

Becky saw Maurie approaching them slowly, as if he didn't want to be involved in their angry encounter. She wanted to avoid speaking to him, so she scurried toward the camp.

11

*F*rom Fort Boise the trail to Oregon no longer followed the Snake River but traversed the barren ranges of the Idaho and Blue Mountains, the final barriers before they reached the Columbia River. The trail across the Blue Mountains proved more difficult than the other mountainous areas—probably due to the physical deterioration of the emigrants and their animals. Each day was a trial to Becky, for the joy and anticipation of their journey was gone, and she suspected that the others felt the same. She no longer had any desire to see Oregon, but she couldn't spend the rest of her life here in this barren wilderness. She had no choice but to go forward.

By now Matt's stock was reduced to three animals, so each day only two mules could be hitched to the wagon. Wagons broke down, causing frequent delays. Two children died. Nothing, however, stopped the procession. In a fit of pique at the heavy toll the trail exacted from travelers, Becky slashed across the one section of unpatched canvas she found on their wagon, OREGON OR DIE TRYING.

Little by little, they overcame every hazard, gradually approaching the snow-covered peaks. The lofty pinnacles hadn't been white when the wagons started toward them, but snow squalls had blanketed the heights.

Becky knew the long journey would end soon, and although she welcomed a cessation of the monotonous days, she wondered what she could do when they reached Oregon. Maurie had made only one attempt to see her since that incident at Fort Boise, and conversation between her and Matt was limited to bare essentials.

Why was I so foolish as to fall in love with him? she asked over and over. She knew Matt well enough to realize that he hadn't seen Maurie as a threat to her, or he wouldn't have permitted any companionship between them. Then why had she allowed herself to dream about him? Even in her innocence, she had known that Maurie's actions had been strange. Yet she had thrown herself at him. She didn't blame Maurie or Matt for her unhappiness; she had brought it all upon herself.

But she did wish she'd listened to Maurie's explanation. After she'd run away from him at the beaver lake, he had followed her to the wagon, Matt right at his heels.

"Becky," he had called, and his voice had sounded desperate. "You must listen to me. It isn't what you think at all."

"She doesn't want to talk to you, Davis; I think she made that plain. And I don't want you to talk to her. Leave us alone. We paid you to guide us to Oregon. After that, I hope Oregon is big enough that we never have to see you again."

Ignoring Matt, Maurie had tried again, "Becky, please talk to me. I can explain everything."

She hadn't answered, and he had gone away. The weeks of silence between them hadn't been easy. Sometimes Becky would see Maurie looking at her, longingly, as if he wanted her to make the first overture, but the hurt was still there—cutting, like a knife twisted in a raw wound. She hated the estrangement on Matt's part, too. Matt had never formed many friendships, and Becky could tell he really liked Maurie, had enjoyed his companionship. But Matt wouldn't admit that either. *Maybe Matt and I are more alike than I thought*, she considered wryly.

More than three weeks elapsed without one word having passed between either of them and Maurie, so Becky was surprised one evening, when they were camped near the top of the last range of mountains, to see Maurie approaching their wagon.

"Becky should have a chance to paint the scene up ahead, and we won't have time to stop in the morning. Do you want to ride up there now?"

Matt stared at him, his hooded eyes devoid of expression. Finally he shrugged his shoulders and turned to Becky, "Do you want to go?"

She nodded slowly, noting that Maurie's face revealed his thoughts no more than Matt's did.

"I'll saddle the horses then."

In a short time, Maurie was leading them toward the mountaintop. Becky patted Beauty encouragingly, noting how gaunt the animal was, praying the horse would live to enjoy a more pleasant existence.

After traveling in silence for over an hour, they rode to the edge of a small meadow, and Becky drew a quick breath. For a moment she couldn't comprehend the magnificent beauty of the panorama spread before them. Ignoring Matt, Maurie dismounted and helped Becky from the saddle. With a wide sweep of his arm, he indicated the scene, speaking softly, "Becky, that's your new home. I wanted to be with you when you saw it for the first time."

Becky's fingers quivered in anticipation of recording such beauty. The sun was slowly dipping behind a range of mountains, dominated by several majestic peaks. One snow-crowned, cone-shaped summit seemed to pierce the darkening sky. The fading sun cast shadows of purple and amber over the vast, arid wasteland that separated the distant mountains from where Becky stood. Below them a wide, turbulent river flowed, having in some bygone era cut its savage course through the barrier of rocks and earth.

"Oh, it's lovely, lovely, Maurie. Tell me what I see."

Matt stood silently observing the mountains, and Maurie spoke softly as Becky's hands outlined the panorama on her sketch pad.

"The big river is the Columbia, which we will reach in a few days. West of us are the Cascade Mountains, which separate us from the Willamette River Valley, and right now, the sun is hovering over the place where our ranch will be."

Our ranch! Whom did he include in the word? His ranch and Luke's? Or could he be thinking . . . ?

"What is the high mountain with all the snow?" Becky queried to check her wayward thoughts.

"That's Mount Hood—there's snow on it all the time. It's probably two hundred miles from here as the crow flies. Farther north, you can see Mount Saint Helens."

"Will we be able to see the mountains from where we're going?"

"If Matt settles in the Willamette Valley, you can see Mount Hood on clear days, although it's about fifty miles east of the Willamette."

Well, so much for her wonderings about "our" ranch.

The three of them watched in silence as Becky completed the initial sketch. By then the sun was almost hidden behind the mountains, having left saffron and mauve streaks in its wake.

When Becky indicated that she was finished, Maurie said, "Now before we go back to the others, both of you are going to listen to what I have to tell you."

Matt started toward his horse. "We don't want to hear it, Davis. Skip it."

"You're going to hear it, if I have to tie you to a tree and make you listen."

"That's easier said than done."

Maurie's voice took on a pleading tone. "I don't want to have trouble with you, Matt, but why can't you be reasonable? Why not give me a chance to defend myself?"

Matt didn't answer, but he leaned against his horse, stiff back showing his displeasure. He made no further move to leave.

Taking Becky's hand, Maurie sat with her on a fallen fir tree. "I don't know why you think I'm so dishonorable that I'd have made love to you when I had no right to do so. I love you, Becky, and I've never loved anyone else. I can't prove that to you, but I'm begging you to take my word for it. Do you believe me?"

Becky nodded, her throat too tight for words.

Maurie directed his words to Matt, "Now about a wife. I was married at one time, but I have a legal divorce." Reaching inside his shirt, he pulled out a paper, which he unfolded and handed to Matt. Matt glanced at it reluctantly, before he returned the paper.

"Bible doesn't recognize divorces, and neither do I. As far as I'm concerned, if you have a living wife, you'll keep away from my sister."

"Your sister might have something to say about that, Matt Miller." Matt ignored her.

"So I'm guilty before I even plead my case, but I'll plead it anyway," Maurie said bitterly.

"I want to hear your story, Maurie; I'm sorry I didn't listen to you three weeks ago."

"I married Rosita Gonzales in New Orleans, after a hasty courtship, when I was eighteen. Too late I learned there was insanity in her family. Rosita's mother had committed suicide when her child was two years old. Rosita was excessively melancholy, and became unreasonably angry and marriage seemed to aggravate her condition. After six months of an impossible marriage, her father had her committed to an asylum.

"That's when I left New Orleans. The lonely trapper's life appealed to me, and occupied as I was with the fight for day-to-day survival, most of the time I could put the past behind me."

He cleared his throat, and Becky recognized the struggle he was having. Had he ever shared this story with anyone before? No one except Luke, she was sure.

"But I couldn't forget those vows I'd taken, 'Till death do us part,' and every few years, I went back to New Orleans, thinking she might have improved. The doctors assured me she would never recover, that she had to be restrained constantly to prevent her from harming herself and others. Her father's considerable estate was providing for her, but I still felt obligated.

"But this past winter," Maurie continued, "when I knew I would probably never return to the East, I went to the asylum to see her. I had to satisfy myself that she was incurable.

"It was the most horrible experience I've ever had. Her body was emaciated, and I could see no trace at all of the woman I'd married. She acted like an animal, and it stunned me to think I was tied to this woman for life. Reluctantly, I accepted the advice of a lawyer and secured a divorce. Not that I thought I'd ever want to marry again, but the lawyer argued that since I was leaving the United States, even if my wife should die, I might never know it. So I do have the divorce."

"I don't think Becky ought to hear this," Matt interrupted.

"I *want* to hear it, Matt. Can't you understand that he has to talk about it? Otherwise, he'll never be rid of the horror of his past."

Maurie gave her a grateful look. "It's true that seeing her brought back all that I'd endured while I lived with Rosita. I was ill-prepared for such a union. Our intimate relations seemed to release a devil in my wife. She was bestial and unreasonable, and if I seemed slow to warm to her embraces, she clawed, bit, abused me, until I hurled her away in disgust. Love was no longer a pure, honorable emotion, but a tainted, sordid nightmare."

Maurie stood and paced before them. Matt was staring at him now, but Becky couldn't see through the tears that blinded her.

"That's why I told Luke I never wanted to touch another woman, and I thought that was true. No woman had stirred my interest, until I saw you, Becky, and even then, at first, I couldn't stand your touch. But your sweet ways, your tenderness, your pure innocence healed me, taught me that there was something beautiful about love, that passion was nothing to be shunned, but a sacred part of the relation between man and that one special woman."

Matt swung into his saddle and rode away, leaving them together. Becky put her arms around Maurie, pulling his head down on her shoulder.

"Maurie, I love you" was all she could think to say, but that seemed to be enough, for she felt the tenseness leave his body.

"I feared to tell you about what had happened to me. That's why I asked you that day at Fort Boise if the drake you mentioned had a broken wing. I've felt like only half a man, one defiled, for so long that I didn't suppose any woman would ever want me."

"I want you, Maurie. What you've told me hasn't changed that."

"But will you want to marry a divorced man, Becky? You deserve better than that."

Becky was slow to answer. "I don't know. This has come too suddenly, and there's something else. You still *feel* married, don't you? Even though you're legally free to marry again, you don't consider yourself free. I'm not sure we could find any happiness that way."

His shoulders slumped as they moved toward the horses, for darkness was creeping across the meadow.

"I'm sorry, but that's true. Nobody made me take those vows that I'd cherish Rosita in sickness and in health and that only death would part us. I wish I didn't feel that way, but I do. Now that I've told you about my past, maybe I'll be able to bury those guilt feelings. Will you wait for me awhile?"

She answered by leaning from her saddle and kissing him.

Matt was sitting on a stool by the wagon, head in his hands when they returned.

"When we reach the Columbia," Maurie said to him, "my obligation to the caravan will be over. Several families plan to go upriver to the Whitman mission, to rest for a few days. Luke and my men will take the cattle and horses overland. He can take your horses, if you want him to. As soon as Reverend Hopkins pays a short visit to the Whitmans, he wants to leave for Oregon City immediately. I've promised to take them by raft. I hope you'll go at the same time, for I don't want Becky on that river with someone who isn't experienced. I know you've lived around rivers all your life, but you haven't seen anything like the Columbia—it's treacherous. Will you go with us?"

Matt nodded curtly, and Becky kissed her fingers, placing them tenderly on Maurie's lips before he walked to his wagon.

All during the ride back with Maurie, Becky had wanted to confide in him about her own past, but she couldn't frame the words. Perhaps even a divorced man wouldn't want her if he knew she'd murdered someone.

"Matt, I want to tell him about Oliver Stover."

Her brother jumped from the stool and pounded the side of the wagon with his fist. With his back to her, he uttered, "Do what you want to. You don't seem to need *my* help anymore."

Becky knew what ailed her brother. He was jealous of Maurie. Touching his arm, she said, "I'm sorry, Matt. You should have known I'd grow up sometime." She stretched a bit to kiss his cheek. Matt stiffened and drew a quick breath; Becky had never kissed him before.

Next morning, Becky rode Beauty and joined Maurie at the head of the caravan.

"You aren't the only one with a past to forget," she began immediately, eager to expunge her memories. "And when you hear what I've done, you may not want me either."

In rapid sentences, she related what had occurred adding, "If I only knew whether or not he died, it might be easier for me, but I don't suppose I'll ever know. As it is, I haven't been able to rid my mind of the burden; I don't think I ever will."

She was encouraged by the compassion in Maurie's eyes. "You should know that wouldn't matter to me. The man, no doubt, needed killing, but it wasn't anything you did deliberately; the shot was an accident he caused himself. I wouldn't worry anymore about it."

"But I've been reminded of the incident several times." Becky told him about the notes on the wagon and the carving on Independence Rock. "Matt and I can't imagine what it all means, but somebody seems intent on harrying us."

"Does seem strange, but let's hope that once we arrive on the other side of those mountains," he gestured toward the Cascade Range, "both of us can forget the past. I'd like to face the future with you, Becky. Otherwise, I'm in for a lonely existence."

"That isn't all, Maurie," Becky said slowly. "You see, my mother wasn't married to my father. That's the reason Matt has been so careful with me. *Like mother, like daughter*, he seems to think. Do you believe I'm wanton?"

She watched his reaction carefully, waiting breathlessly for his words, which came quickly.

"Of course, you're not wanton! Did Matt say you were?"

"I've heard it from his lips for years, but I didn't know until after we started on this trip why he thought that. Do you think I could have inherited my mother's weaknesses?"

"Matt Miller is crazy for worrying you like that. I suppose we do inherit the poorer traits of our ancestors, but we inherit their strong points, too. Dwell on those, Becky. You don't have anything to be ashamed of. As long as you're determined, you can be the kind of person you want to be, regardless of what your parents did."

His words erased forever the shame of Becky's past.

The descent into the Columbia Valley was as treacherous as any part of the trail. The way was narrow and steep, the worn wagon brakes would seldom hold, and on the sheerest inclines, the drivers tied ropes around the wagons, anchored them to huge fir trees, and eased them slowly over the mountains.

Those final days were nerve-racking to everyone, and when they finally drew their wagons to a halt on the banks of the boisterous Columbia, Becky couldn't believe that they'd finally reached the end of the trail. She watched her fellow travelers as the truth dawned on them that, in spite of the odds against them, they'd made it over the Oregon Trail.

The children yelled joyously, and Shoshone barked loudly, as though he sensed the relief of his human companions. Reverend and Mrs. Hopkins stood arm in arm, praying silently. Susie stood beside them, the tears flowing. Matt noisily cleared his throat, and Maurie dropped to his knees, eyes closed, lips moving silently. Becky went to kneel beside him, and when he lifted his head, he drew her to him, kissing her willing lips.

While the Hopkinses and Becky went to the Whitman mission, Maurie and Luke helped Matt build a raft from the tall fir trees growing near the river. In three days, they were ready to complete the final phase of their journey.

Becky helped Matt wrap their few possessions in skins, to protect them from moisture on the raft. Encasing the steamboat whistle in a crate, he said, "Becky, thank you for bringing the whistle. It does mean a lot to me."

"Sure, Matt. It means a lot to me, too. I want you to

have it for your first steamboat out here. You haven't given up that dream, have you?"

"No, but from the looks of this river, I may have to wait a while."

Matt had dismantled the wagon to make a little cabin on the raft, for the comfort of the women on the three-day trip to Oregon City. He was sending his mules and horses with Luke.

Maurie, working on the other end of the raft, called, "What are you going to do about Shoshone, Becky? He won't like the raft."

"Wonder if Rusty would mind taking him on the trail with the cattle? We could fetch Shoshone to Oregon City as soon as we're settled."

"Good idea," Maurie agreed, and Becky suspected that was what he'd had in mind all along. "The fellows won't have an easy time of it, for there's no trail at all, but Luke thinks he can make it. Maybe it's a good thing there are only fifteen of the cattle left."

"It's too bad so many of them died, but at least you have a few left to start your herd."

As confident as she was in Maurie's ability, Becky was shaking inwardly when they shoved their craft into the swirling current of the Columbia. The faces of the other passengers were wary, but no one questioned Maurie's plans until they came to a string of rapids where the steep cliffs pressed in on both sides. The gorge ahead was narrow and crooked, and the water tempestuous.

"Maurie, is this safe?" Reverend Hopkins asked.

"No," Maurie answered honestly, "but the cliffs here won't allow a portage, and there's no other way to go through. Many travelers have navigated these rapids, and

I think we'll make it. But don't anyone get skittish and try to leave the raft."

Matt and Maurie picked up long poles to guide the raft, and the women huddled in the center. "Want to go inside the cabin?" Matt asked Becky.

She shook her head. Though she was terrified, she wanted to see what was happening. But when the raging water claimed their small craft, Becky clamped her eyes shut and held on for dear life. The raft twisted and creaked; she was drenched with the roaring water that deafened her; but soon the raft flowed into smoother water.

"We made it," Maurie shouted in exaltation.

Wide-eyed, Susie said, "I liked that. Wasn't it fun?"

Becky said nothing, but she patted her waist, to reassure herself that the packet for the provisional government was still there. In the height of danger on the rapids, she hadn't feared for her own life as much as she dreaded having Aunt Lizzie's mission fail within a few days of Oregon City.

Except for occasional rapids, the river was smoother after that, and Becky enjoyed the swift, scenic trip downstream. The river was lined with tall, evergreen trees, and beyond the forests, she glimpsed broad meadows gleaming in the sunlight.

Six months to the day from the time they left Independence, the buildings of Fort Vancouver, the Hudson's Bay Company's headquarters, came into view. Maurie and Matt poled the raft from the Columbia into the Willamette, which was calm in comparison to the river they'd traveled on for three days.

Becky breathed in relief when she finally stepped ashore

at Oregon City. Turning to Maurie she said, "Will you tell me where I can find George Abernethy?"

"Why would you want to see him?"

Smothering a smile, Becky said calmly, "He's head of Oregon's provisional government, isn't he? I have a message for him."

If Becky had ever hoped to have revenge against Matt for the many years of domination, that would have been her supreme moment. But many miles back along the trail, she had forgiven her brother. Slowly Matt comprehended what she had said, his mottled face a puzzle. Matt Miller would never again take his sister for granted.

12

Becky suspected Maurie was irritated, but without asking any questions, he motioned her to follow him. Matt plodded silently behind them.

Wedged in between an abrupt bluff and the Willamette River, Oregon City appeared to be a busy town. Becky noted a small stockade, over which a Hudson's Bay Company flag snapped in the breeze. They passed a Methodist church, and a few unpretentious structures before Maurie stopped in front of a brick building.

"George Abernethy is the owner of this missionary store. He should be inside. Do you want to go in alone?"

She shook her head vigorously. "No, you come with me."

"You seemed to have managed by yourself this far," he said, and she knew he was annoyed because she hadn't confided in him.

"Matt, you come with me then," she asked, but both men followed her into the store.

"Mr. Abernethy is upstairs," the clerk behind the counter told them motioning them toward a rickety stairway.

Inside the stairwell, Becky said, "Turn your heads a minute," and she lifted her skirts to unfasten the heavy belt. In more ways than one, she felt as if a weight had been lifted from her person.

Confronting George Abernethy in his tiny room, Becky laid the leather belt on his desk. "That was sent to you by James K. Polk. I'm not sure what's in it, but I think the letter will explain."

"James K. Polk?" Abernethy said. "The one who's likely to become president of the United States."

Becky nodded. "That's the one."

Glancing at Maurie, whom he recognized, Abernethy quickly untied the thongs fastening the belt. Becky heard Matt groan when a wad of money was revealed. Abernethy counted the bills quickly, and whistled. "Twenty thousand dollars! Young woman, you've been a walking bank." Matt sat down on a nearby chair, as if his legs wouldn't hold him any longer.

A letter was enclosed with the money:

To the American Settlers in Oregon:

Help is on the way. Hold on for another few months. If I'm successful in being elected president of the United States, I can assure you that I will do everything in my power to bring Oregon under the American flag. This continent will one day belong to the United States—from the Atlantic to the Pacific.

Backers of "54° 40' or Fight" have raised the enclosed money to help you arm for conflict, if negotiations do not succeed.

You will hear more from us in the near future. Oregon for American settlers!

James K. Polk

Abernethy's face was wreathed in smiles. "Young lady, this news couldn't have come at a better time. In the past two weeks, we've been barraged by a few newcomers who have taunted us about our right to Oregon. They claimed they'd come from the United States government to tell us of a new joint-occupation agreement with the British. We were just about ready to declare Oregon an independent country and fight the British by ourselves."

"One of the men called Hudnall, by any chance?" Maurie asked.

"That's right," Abernethy said. "Tall man with a limp. Did you encounter him on the trail?"

Briefly Maurie told of their troubles with Hudnall and his companions, adding, "If they did scatter many guns among the Indians, that money you've received will come in handy. We may have a fight on our hands."

"We?" Abernethy said. "If I remember, last fall, you were one of the men who counseled that we should continue joint occupation with the British."

"That's true, but since then I've changed my mind. I'll support only American sovereignty over Oregon from now on."

Abernethy turned to Becky again. "May I ask how you came to have this packet, miss? It seems strange that Mr. Polk would entrust such a message to you."

"I've never seen Mr. Polk," and with pride in her voice, she told him about Aunt Lizzie and her valiant effort to complete the mission. "Since she knew her chances for finishing the journey were slim, she had to have someone else to take over. She swore me to secrecy." Becky looked beseechingly at Matt and Maurie. "That's the reason I didn't tell either of you. I promised at her deathbed that I'd not tell."

Becky's friends were soon caught up in the spirit of progress prevailing in the settlement. Reverend Hopkins and the Leviatt brothers each filed on a square mile of land within a week, and while the minister built a home for his family and made plans for his new mission, he lodged his wife and daughter in a boardinghouse near the river. Matt rented a room for Becky next to theirs.

As soon as he had seen Becky settled, Maurie had left town, expecting to meet Luke at his ranch. That had been a month ago, and Becky hadn't heard from him since. A few hurried minutes alone with him, before his departure, just allowed time for a quick kiss and his whispered, "Oh, Becky, I wish I could take you with me."

Although Matt was forced to admit that his dream of a steamboat was a long way off, he had started a river business; using the raft built for their journey down the Columbia, he hauled supplies the thirteen miles from Portland, by the mouth of the Willamette to Oregon City. Ocean-going vessels navigated the Columbia up to the Willamette, and the people of Oregon City needed their goods.

Determined to be free from Matt's domination, Becky declared her intention to provide for herself. Since Maurie felt bound by his former marriage, she wasn't sure she had any future with him, but she could still pursue her own happiness. If this man had no place in her life, then God had something else for her.

The packet of drawings was already on its way to Hamilton, for she had entrusted them to the captain of a sailing vessel going around the Horn to New Orleans. Matt had asked to see her paintings before she packaged them, and he shook his head, a resigned look on his newly shaven face, when he saw how often Maurie appeared in her artwork.

"Becky, no man is worth all that adoration."

"That's the way it is, Matt; I can't help it."

Matt's fingers threaded his hair, and he muttered, "I'm beginning to wish I had someone who loved me like that."

He flushed as he said it, and Becky laughed. "Maybe you're human after all, Brother."

"It isn't funny, Becky. After we had that quarrel at Fort Boise, I finally accepted that you would go with Maurie. I've been miserable since then. When neither you nor Maurie would talk to me, I had lots of time to think."

Knowing she was on the point of a new relationship with Matt, Becky sat down, waiting quietly.

"If I'd lost you, Becky, I'd have had nothing. Not even any pleasant thoughts of the past. It's a devilish situation for a grown man to realize that he's wasted most of his life in hating. I know my relentlessness made Mom's last days miserable. I can't tell her that I've forgiven her, but I want you to know it."

"Matt, I'm glad you've told me."

"My view of God has even changed. I used to think of God as a vengeful Sovereign." Matt's eyes took on a wondering aspect as he continued, "Then I realized that *Jesus* had demonstrated God's true nature. When I thought how Jesus had told that prostitute, 'Neither do I condemn thee; go, and sin no more,' I understood how wrong I'd been. God loves us in spite of our shortcomings."

Becky laid her head against Matt's chest, and he placed his arm around her, holding her awkwardly.

"I understand the struggle you've had, Matt. After Aunt

Lizzie told me that I was a bastard, for days I was belligerent toward everyone. I hated my parents intensely. But if Maurie hadn't been stronger than I, the same thing could have happened to me. I don't feel hatred for anyone now—not even Oliver Stover or Hudnall."

"Well, I haven't advanced to that point yet," Matt said as he released her. "I'm afraid I won't be accountable for my actions if I ever run into Hudnall."

Since many months would elapse before she heard from Hamilton, looking for some means of support until she received payment for her sketches, Becky went to work at the boardinghouse. When she wasn't working, she and Susie tried to replenish their wardrobes. Fabrics were scarce and expensive in Oregon City, but they had found a few yards of material, which they stitched into new dresses.

However much it might have hurt him, Matt stayed away from her for two weeks, but when he came and saw her waiting on tables, he glowered throughout his meal. Later, in her room, he said, "Please, Becky, don't work here. I won't boss you around anymore if you'll let me provide for you. I'm fond of you, Sister, you know that."

Brushing her hair before a cracked mirror, Becky said, "I know that, Matt; you've been good to me in your way, but I've made up my mind. I hope we can be friends, but I'm making my own decisions from now on."

"Does that mean you're going to marry Maurie?"

"I don't know. I think he has the same idea about re-marriage that you have, but I wasn't referring to that. I may not marry anyone."

Matt snorted. "In a place like this, where there are about a dozen men to one woman, you'll have to marry somebody, especially since everyone knows about your bringing that packet to Abernethy. You're the talk of the town."

She smiled, thinking how Aunt Lizzie had predicted that Becky would be in history books if she completed her mission.

He looked at her steadily. "You didn't look like much when we arrived here, but you're prettier than ever now. I reckon a month of rest was all you needed. You're not so skinny, and your hair and skin are soft again. Every unattached man will be eyeing you, now that you won't let me protect you, so I hope you'll be careful."

Becky looked at him, mouth agape. Matt had told her she was pretty, was actually extolling her virtues. Life on the trail had changed her brother!

"Well, at least," he said, rising, "come down to the river with me. I brought up some silk cloth that came on a ship from China, and I want you to have your pick before I take it to the stores. Ask Susie to come along, too, and she can select something."

The three of them passed through the small town, which Becky eyed with interest, because she hadn't ventured out alone, an action Matt definitely approved. Pausing to sample some smoked salmon that a native was offering for sale, Becky saw Maurie swinging down the street.

He hailed them happily. "Just came to town a few minutes ago, and here I run into you." Matt didn't seem overjoyed to see him.

"Did Rusty arrive at the ranch with Shoshone? Is he all right?"

Rubbing his unshaven face, Maurie said, "Sure did, but I didn't bring the dog along this time—didn't know what you'd do with him here. He's all right where he is now. Rusty'll look out for him."

"Hudnall," Matt alerted them as he observed a group of men across the street in front of a saloon.

Hudnall hadn't seen them yet, but Becky wasn't interested in him anyway. *Who is the man standing beside Hudnall?* His back was turned, but somehow he seemed familiar, and when he faced them, Becky had a queasy feeling clear from her stomach to the top of her head. She grabbed Matt's arm, afraid, until it dawned on her that she wasn't seeing the ghost of the man who had haunted her for six months; it was Oliver Stover himself.

"Stover!" Matt muttered, recognizing him soon after she did.

A flood of thanksgiving rushed over Becky to finally know that she hadn't killed the man, but she immediately wondered what Oliver was doing here in Oregon City and if he could take any action against her for that affair on the *Allegheny.*

"Just a minute, Miller," Stover called as he saw them.

Oliver hurried their way, his face wearing that sadistic, superior smile Becky despised. "Now, isn't this a pleasant surprise to find Matt Miller and his pretty little sister out here in Oregon." Becky sensed that he wasn't surprised at all; somehow he had discovered their destination and followed them. Since he was with Hudnall, she surmised Oliver had been traveling with that group. No doubt he was responsible for the signs on their wagon and the inscriptions on Independence Rock.

Hudnall joined Oliver, saying, "Well, here's the little heroine herself! Just about as famous as Joan of Arc—carrying a message of hope across the continent."

"Knock it off, Hudnall," Maurie entered the conversation. "Everybody knows what you birds are trying to do. If you're so keen on the British, go to Fort Vancouver. You're not welcome in Oregon City."

"Prove it, Davis, just try to prove it," Hudnall said, and his hand dropped to the pocket of his coat.

"Are you going to have a fight?" Susie asked. "If you are, I'm going back to the boardinghouse. Mother will have a fit, if I'm mixed up in one."

"No, there's not going to be a fight," Matt said, pushing Hudnall to one side. "Not unless they start something. I've had enough of you two skunks to last a lifetime. Let's go, girls."

Hudnall and Stover watched them go, but not without a last word. "It's a good thing for you, Miss Heroine, that we didn't know you were the one bringing the message," Oliver jeered, but the words had no effect on Becky now.

"Think we've heard the last of them, Maurie?" Matt inquired. The wooden walkway was narrow, and Susie walked beside Matt, while Maurie and Becky followed.

"I figure they'll hang around for a while, but thanks to Becky's action, no one is paying any attention to them anymore." Turning to Becky, Maurie asked quietly, so his words wouldn't reach Susie's ears, "Is Stover the man you shot, Becky?"

"Yes, and it's a relief to know I don't have his murder hanging over me. Knowing Matt, he won't put up with any sass from Oliver."

Passing a shack that served as a warehouse for ocean shipping, an old man hailed them, "Hey, ain't you Maurie Davis?"

"It'll be dark before we get to the raft," Matt muttered.

Maurie acknowledged his identity, while the man squinted at him, shading his eyes from the piercing rays of the setting sun.

"Thought you were. Remembered seeing you when you were here a year ago. Well, we got a whole passel of boxes for you. Came all the way from New Orleans, they did."

"These must be the seeds and household goods I had shipped before I left New Orleans last spring. They made good time." The four of them went into the building.

"Seems like everything is here," Maurie said, "but I can't take them for a few days. I'll make arrangements soon to haul these to my property upriver. My mother's furniture will look odd in that little log cabin, but at least I'll feel at home."

When they were on the verge of leaving, the man halted them again while he rummaged in a box of papers, drawing out a letter.

"This is for you, too. The captain of the bark gave it to me and said to be sure you got it. Special, he said."

Outside the building, Maurie turned the letter over in his hand, and Becky noted the color receding from his face. "It's from the institution where Rosita is a patient," he said. "I left my forwarding address with the superintendent." He placed the letter in his pocket.

"Aren't you going to open it?"

His face was white, and she knew he was reliving the horror of his marriage. "I can't, Becky."

Sensing his despair, Becky was glad for Susie's chatter as they neared Matt's raft. Becky had suddenly lost interest in new clothes, but to make her brother happy, she chose two pieces of silk that would make beautiful garments.

"I'll only take enough for one, Matt, and it's generous of you to give me this," Susie said. "Everything is scarce in Oregon City—money especially."

The letter in Maurie's pocket was as vivid to Becky as if she could see it as they moseyed back toward town.

"Come on up to my room," she invited Matt and Maurie, in front of the boardinghouse. "We can visit until I go to work in about an hour."

Becky perched on the bed, to leave the two straight chairs for Maurie and Matt. Maurie didn't have his mind on visiting, and while he sat on the rustic wooden chair, he looked at the letter again.

"Kinda strange," he said. "A man who has enough nerve to pilot a bunch of emigrants across the continent, but is still too much of a coward to open a letter." Recklessly he slashed the seal of the letter with his fingernail.

Becky watched his expression as he read, thinking his face couldn't become any whiter, but it did. His eyes caught Becky's, and she saw hope dawning on his face as he handed the letter to Matt.

"Mr. Davis," Matt read aloud.

It is my sad duty to inform you that five days after you left New Orleans, your wife, Rosita, died. I sent a letter to Independence, but in the event you didn't receive it, I'm sending a duplicate letter to Oregon.

I am sorry for the many unhappy memories you have had to bear, and I pray that the future will make up for your past sorrows.

Matt folded the letter carefully and returned it to Maurie. Not a sound could be heard in the room, and Becky found it difficult to breathe. What if Maurie had received his letter in Independence? How much different their relationship might have been! But she breathed more easily when she realized that Maurie was free at last—his marriage had been dissolved in the scriptural way. Surely this would wipe away his unhappiness.

Becky looked at Matt, wondering what he thought, but as usual his face was inscrutable.

"Well, Matt?" Maurie said.

Matt cleared his throat several times before he managed

to say, "She's making her own decisions now, Davis, so it isn't up to me. But let me tell you what I think." Becky waited tensely, watching in amazement as a beautiful smile overspread Matt's face. "No man on earth is good enough for her, but you come nearer to measuring up than anyone else I've ever known. So if you want each other, you have my blessing."

Maurie rose to meet Matt halfway, and their hands clasped. Becky jumped off the bed and ran to them, throwing her arms first around Matt and then flinging herself into Maurie's waiting arms, offering him her lips.

God *had* given her the desires of her heart.